Portal of Ruin

Copyright © 2023 A.N. Sage

PORTAL
OF RUIN

A.N. SAGE

OLIVERHEBERBOOKS

CONTENTS

Chapter One

Billie

*T*he air sparkled, an unnatural sparkle that filled the graveyard, and made my eyes blink wildly as I gathered the last of my strength. I fisted my hands, pressing them tightly into my sides and shutting my eyes as I willed myself to keep going. Behind me muffled voices rose as I shook my head, trying to concentrate on the task at hand.

Deep inside my belly, the shadows growled as they came to life. My legs buckled, and I stumbled ever so slightly. Within seconds, a strong palm pressed to my back, holding me steady. *River,* I thought. *Always there when I need him.*

With a renewed sense of duty, I refocused my intentions and uncurled my fingers, slamming my palms forward and letting the shadows loose. They swarmed the space between my body and where the portal once stood, twisting and twirling, looking for something that wasn't there. I gritted my teeth, brow slick with sweat, and kept pushing. The tornado of darkness in front of me widened and overtook almost the entire cemetery. Shouts rose behind me, and this time I did not push them out. I had to stop before I destroyed everything with my magic.

Willing the shadows back in, I shook my head, wiped my brow, and turned to my friends. "This isn't working!"

"Don't give up so easily. Keep trying!" Rhiamon shouted.

The high priestess rarely spoke, yet when she did, it was to offer a command. Today was no different. She ran a hand over the sword she often carried and flipped her long braids over a muscular shoulder, piercing me with a serious glare. After spending the first portion of my life in the High Coven, I knew the look Rhiamon sported meant business. It also meant I had to hurry my butt up and do something.

I closed my eyes. It wasn't easy to stay calm when there was no turning back. And when there was nothing we could do to stop whatever crazy plan Cathan, my fae father, had set in motion. My eyes blinked wildly, pushing away the tears welling in my eyes. River was right; I had to keep trying. We couldn't just leave our friends in Faerie, could we? There was no world in which I could let my half-brother, Logan, rot in that place. And what about the girls? Certainly, they only volunteered to keep him company. I wasn't sure what Vic's situation was or why she decided to stay behind. But I knew for certain Savannah only stayed for Logan, her boyfriend. Now she'd be stuck there forever because of me. Because I didn't have the guts to kill Cathan when I had the chance.

I bet this wasn't the family reunion Logan had in mind when he met me a year ago and realized we were related.

I sighed, trying to gulp air that was hard to come by. My hands formed into fists once again. Deep inside, the shadows rustled, overtaking my body. They were ready to fight. They were ready to try. Was I? I wasn't so sure anymore. My feet shook in my boots as I dug my heels into the ground to put on some air of bravado. I paused and looked over my shoulder to see the high priestesses glare me down. Watching my mother stand beside them was baffling. I never thought I'd see those witches together. Beatrix smiled that same smile I remembered from when I was a kid, and you would think it would give me more courage, but all it did was remind me I wasn't good enough to accomplish this. That I wasn't good enough to save our friends or the rest of the world. That all I could do was trap Cathan, and I didn't even do that by myself.

It took the High Coven and the rogues almost two weeks to figure out how to store my bastard father. Turns out even in shadow form Cathan was impossible to keep down. After nearly giving up, the rogues came up with a solution that even Sebyl had to admit was creative. They gathered up everything which was Cathan—all the shadow magic, all the spirit energy, everything I poured into him, and everything he poured into himself trying to escape—and they trapped the idiot in a bottle. Like a damn genie. I could laugh over it, if every once in a while I didn't think someone might come along, rub the bottle, and let the genie out.

In the end, we got it done. Well, *they* did. Two weeks working with the rogues and it seemed the High Coven was starting to come around. For a moment there, I actually thought Sebyl might have enjoyed working with them. I knew she wouldn't ever admit it, but the rogues were powerful witches, and their refusal to use magic by the coven's rules made them even stronger. They were creative and thought outside the box. Something Sebyl would probably never do. Though, if I thought about Cathan sitting in the bottle, huffing and puffing in his shadow form, maybe I was wrong. Maybe even Sebyl had a bit of rebellion in her.

I pulled the loose shadows dangling at the edge of my

fingertips back inside, leaned on River, and faced the others. "I don't think we're doing this the right way. We keep pushing and pushing, but clearly, force is not the way to get the portal open."

"So, what do you suggest?" asked Sebyl. Her blunt bob framed the sharp angles of her face, drawing my attention to her thin lips. "We've tried everything and nothing has worked. If it is not by force, then how do we knock the door wide open to save your friends?" The intonation of her voice on 'save your friends' made me roll my eyes. Sebyl didn't care about saving anyone. All she cared about was getting rid of the enemy we shared so she could keep the power she once held over the supernaturals. Well, I wasn't gonna let her do that. Though that didn't mean I wasn't going to play along for a while. I needed the grumpy old witch.

Sebyl grimaced, her dark, painted eyes narrowing, as she tried to figure out what I was up to. *Good luck, Sebyl. I don't even know what I'm up to yet.*

In my mind, River growled through our bond. *"Take it easy. No need to start a war yet."*

I turned to face him, those piercing green eyes undoing me. Today, his brown hair was tousled, and I could see that dimple that made me smile make an appearance. Taking small, steady breaths to regain my composure, I rolled my shoulders and said, "There has to be a spell we can try. Something intricate. Something small. Something we wouldn't think to use."

"We tried it all and nothing worked," my mother said. "I think Sebyl is right on this. If we can't take this portal by force, we might not be able to take it at all."

"No! Absolutely no way!" I shouted. "We are not leaving them there. Besides, without getting the portal open, we might never find out what Cathan planned, and I think we all know that the bastard had a lot more coming. Sure, we caught him, but he's not letting himself stay trapped. Something is still coming. I can feel it in the air. He's not done. And if *he's* not done, then *we* are not done trying to stop him. The only way to do that is to open this stupid portal." Sweat pooled on my neck and I brushed it off. "I know you all think I'm only doing this to save my friends, but that is not true. If I'm right, we have a lot more to worry about. We have the whole world to worry about."

This time my body vibrated as my magic started to take form. It scared me a little how out of control I'd been feeling lately. It seemed that every time I tried to use my magic, the shadows would take over. It was nearly impossible for me to capture any other elements. I even tried crystals, herbs, potions, anything I could get my hands on, and the shadows always took control. As though once I used them to trap Cathan, something got set free. Some beast inside of me I didn't know existed. And since I didn't know it existed, I couldn't keep it chained fast enough. Now, most of the time, I felt made almost entirely of shadow. It was in the air I breathed, the water I drank. It was in the sunshine. Darkness. Always darkness.

You want force, I thought. *I'll give you force.* I threw my palms out, ramming them through the space where the portal once was. A black tornado poured from my fingertips and twined over my arms and my legs, the energy of it almost too much to bear. Holding on to the shadows like one would hold on to a big hound, I zeroed them in on the portal site, trying to coat as much of the air with my magic as possible. My rubbery legs shook uncontrollably, knees knocking, sweat dripping down the insides of my thighs. Everything in my body felt like it was on fire. I was burning and I couldn't stop it. Not until I was satisfied.

River said something, but I couldn't hear him because words didn't make sense. Nothing made sense anymore. My eyes snapped wide open; a bright glow emanating from them and piercing through the darkness. I twirled my fingertips, pushing more magic to pour out of me—almost hoping that enough would pour out and I would never have magic again.

My eyes widened to saucers and for a second, I thought I felt the air ripple, but it was only sweat falling into my eyes. I let myself relax as my magic climbed back inside. "See," I said, "force doesn't work." Then added, "Not everything can just be taken because we want it."

The high priestess's lips formed this thin line, but to my surprise, she didn't utter a word.

"I think that's enough, babe," River said. "Should we head home for the day? You can take a look at the Book of Darkness, see if you missed something. You're gonna run yourself into the ground if you keep pushing."

He was right; River was always right. He knew when I've had enough and he knew that if I kept going, it will be bad for everyone. But I definitely wasn't going back home— wherever that was now. Most of my free time was spent between the resistance and the townhouse. Since Beatrix moved in with the High Coven to help Luna scour the library for spells, it made sense to visit often.

"I want to try the caves again," I told River. "I'm not going home right now."

"What do you think you'll find there that we haven't found already? Billie, you've been in those caves at least three times and came up empty. Cathan didn't hide some map to his secret plan in there."

"Well, he must have hidden it somewhere!"

"Why? Why would he do that? Why would anyone who's as clever and vile as him leave any trace of his vicious plans around?"

I sighed. "Because of his evil, River. I know him. I know what he's like. He is so cocky he would actually think that he could write his damn plans across the sky and nobody would figure it out. There has to be something, if not his plan, then perhaps there's something we missed about opening the portal. We did it before."

"Before you had Logan," River reminded me. Like I required the reminder; I knew I needed my brother's spirit magic to help me. As strong as I felt on my own, having his magic combined with mine, well, the portal probably would have been open by now.

"I can't go home," I said, shaking my head.

"Okay, where do you want to go?"

"Let's try the Crystal Cauldron. Ms. Broussard might have come up with something while we were gone. If anything, I could use the crystals to recharge."

River grinned from ear to ear. "That peppermint tea she makes does sound pretty great right about now."

I chuckled. "You're always so easy to tempt."

River wrapped his arm around me and I melted into him. My mate marks crawled higher up my arms in response to his body being so close. My head felt suddenly heavy, and I couldn't wait to get into his car and take a quick snooze on the way to Main Street. I looked up at River. "You think they're doing okay over there?"

"If I know anything about those three, they're doing fine. They're probably trying to figure this crap out on their own."

"I hope you're right," I whispered. "I hope they figure it out. Because we sure can't."

"I'm sure they will. Give it time."

I stifled a laugh. Time was something we didn't have. I don't know how I knew it, but I felt something was coming for all of us, something big and wretched and dirty. I wish I knew what it was.

My stomach growled as River tugged me along. "Let's go! A tired Billie is one thing, but a tired and *hungry* Billie... well, let's say I'm not ready to face that today!"

I grazed my mother's shoulder with my palm. "Call you if we find anything," I told her.

As we walked through the graveyard, my eyes darted between the tombstones, taking in all the names of the witches long passed. *I won't let you down,* I thought. *I'll figure this out.*

Deep down, I knew I was lying. I might never figure this out. Our only hope now was that Logan was faring better on the other side of the portal, or else we'd all be doomed.

Chapter Two

Logan

"I hate this bloody realm!" I shook my leg as the slimy substance on it dripped down like molasses and hit the purple ground with a slop. My stomach turned. I tied my long hair up in a bun and brushed the remainder of the nasty substance from my silk pants. "This is probably the grossest sodding thing I've ever experienced."

Beside me, Savannah laughed, and the sharp sound of her voice made me laugh as well. "Don't be such a wuss," she said, barely able to contain her laughter. "It's just a little tree sap."

I looked down at my soaked leg. "It looks like a lot more than a little tree sap..."

Savannah's cheeks burned, and I immediately regretted embarrassing her. Though I had to admit that Savannah's blushing made me want to do it that much more. Her long curls brushed against her collarbone, and I immediately wanted to reach out and touch her. The tight fae bodysuit accentuating every curve of her body didn't help. With a groan, I crawled out from inside the tree and rolled my shoulders.

"You sure this is what Waverly asked for?" I asked.

I held up the very regular, very boring rock I acquired from within so Savannah could see it. She inspected it quickly, then nodded. "That's the one."

I had no idea what this rock had to do with us finding our way out of this bloody realm. It had been almost a year here —merely several weeks in Shadowhurst—but a full year in Faerie. Even with Savannah here and Victoria, well, sort of here, I was going out of my wretched mind. I glanced at Savannah, her one-piece suit tightly clinging to her very fit body, and shook my head. *Only a real plonker would regret spending a year trapped in a magical realm with this goddess.* I supposed that's what I had become in Faerie: a bloody plonker. My body shook with a heavy sigh as I tossed the rock in the air, catching it and cramming it into my trousers' pocket. "Let's get this over with," I said. "Whatever Waverly has planned, I'm certain it can't wait, as always."

The one thing the fae had going for her was her impatience. Anyone else would have been annoyed by it, but I actually enjoyed that part of Waverly's personality. It meant that she would do whatever it took to get us out of here. Except, so far, everything she attempted hadn't worked, and we were still stuck in this dodgy realm. Every attempt we'd made at opening the portal had failed. Even Victoria, who was pretty much the strongest witch I'd met other than Billie, couldn't figure it out. Of course, she'd have to be around for me to know if she was actually doing something. Since we realized there might not be a going-home for any of us, Victoria all but disappeared off the face of the planet. It was bloody infuriating. Each time I needed advice from someone who actually knew something about witch magic, she was nowhere to be found. She'd try to make up for it later, showing up at the palace with some brilliant new idea to try. I had no clue how she came up with any of it, because these were spells that even Billie wouldn't have thought of. They relied on using the realm's magic in ways most witches wouldn't know how to use, ways outside of crystals and herbs and things found in nature. It was as though Victoria was learning how to tap into the realm using only her own energy. We all knew that Faerie was special for witches, allowed them to use their magic without needing conduits, but what Victoria was doing... it was something entirely different. She wasn't using the energy in Faerie, she was changing it, somehow tailoring the realm to fit whatever she needed.

Each time she tried one of her so-called spells, I felt the realm shift. I worried one day she might break Faerie to pieces, and since we had no way out, we'd be screwed. What a cock-up that would be.

This morning when Waverly asked us to look for some magical rock, I knew immediately the entire plan had Victoria written all over it. The witch thought of something else. I wish I knew how she did it. *Must have something to do with the water fae she'd been spending her time with.* I'd only seen the bloke once, and Solen seemed like a decent guy, but something about him didn't sit right—like he had filthy secrets to hide.

"Did you hear anything I said?" Savannah asked.

Bloody hell. I really didn't. I smiled. "Sorry, love. Got into my own head."

"Well, don't be such a... what do you call it?"

"A tosser," I offered.

"Yeah, that. Don't be that."

I saluted her like a soldier. "All right, I'm all yours!"

Savannah jabbed me with her elbow and smiled. "Let's get this thing to Waverly and see what she can cook up."

Waverly turned the rock over carefully, her long fingertips poking at every nook and cranny, and for a second there, I thought we got the wrong one. She ran a finger over the small horns protruding from her head, tapping the end of one. When she finally released the stone and placed it in the center of the circle cast on the ground, my shoulders sagged. "Care to explain what this is for?" I asked.

"Something your witch came up with," Waverly answered. "She's clever, that one. I wouldn't have thought to do this myself."

I shot Savannah my best 'I told you so' look and chuckled when she rolled her eyes.

Waverly moved the rock over an inch and stepped out of the circle. It was strange to see a circle in the middle of Faerie, where magic grew itself from the ground like grass, but there it was, plunked down for everyone to see.

"The witch thinks we can use Earth magic here to transfer the energy. Make it so that the portal thinks it's being opened from both sides."

"That sounds like a stretch."

Savannah's ears perked up beside me. "What makes Victoria think this can work?"

"I would assume Solen had something to do with it," Waverly said.

My eyebrows slanted. "The water fae?"

She nodded. "Oh, Solen is much more than a simple water fae," she said, but didn't offer further explanation. I was pied off in my own realm. I assumed Waverly thought I knew more about this Solen character, considering that I was supposed to be the fae's bloody king. In my defense, I barely knew the guy except for what Victoria told us, which was nearly nothing.

"And what do Solen and Victoria think this little rock can do?" I asked.

Waverly tossed a fast glance at the rock. "It isn't a rock."

"If it looks like a rock and quacks like a rock," Savannah whispered.

Luckily, Waverly didn't hear her and said, "This is an Earth rock."

"I'm sorry, did you say an Earth rock? What on Earth is the Earth rock doing here?" Savannah screeched.

Blimey. This was not good; I could feel it. Any time something from Earth made its way to Faerie, all hell broke loose. Savannah and I being here was prime example of that. The two realms had no business mixing and nothing could convince me otherwise.

Waverly blinked her golden eyes. "A long time ago, that fool Cathan began bringing things from Earth back here. He thought they would somehow help open the portal from our side, or at least give us control of it. It didn't work, of course. But now we have pieces of your Earth all over all our realm, tucked away for safekeeping."

I glanced at the rock that now looked a lot less bland than it did before. My eyes darted from the it to Savannah as she said, "If it didn't work for Cathan, what makes you think it will work for us?"

Waverly shrugged. "Nothing, but your witch seems to

think otherwise, and at this point, we'd be fools not to give it a try."

"Everyone ready?" A bell-like voice sounded from the trees; I turned on my heels to see Victoria standing next to Solen behind us. They were only an inch apart, and I could have sworn I saw her yank her hand away from his as soon as our eyes made contact.

I ran a hand through my long hair. "So, what is the plan here? What do you want to do with the Earth rock?"

Without bothering to answer, Victoria brushed past me and knelt next to the circle. Her fingertips buried in the ground all the way up to her knuckles like she was digging for treasure. Her eyes shut, lids fluttering as she recited words I could not understand over and over again. With every incantation I felt Faerie shift. It was as though the air thickened when Victoria performed this new mangled form of magic. In the center of the circle, the rock began to glow, no longer gray, but a bright shade of pink. As its light intensified, I watched it hover off the ground, rising higher and higher. Beneath it, the air rippled, looking an awful like a portal starting to form. I held my breath. *This is it. The witch might actually do it this time.*

As soon as I thought it, the rock dimmed and dropped to the ground with a thud.

I looked at Victoria, her face red and her arms shaking. "You alright?"

Victoria nodded, gutted. "It didn't work."

As the witch rose to stand, Savannah's soft fingers intertwined in mine and I took a step back from the circle. Perhaps it was time to admit it—we were never going back to Shadowhurst. We were never going home. All I could do was hope that my sister found a way to end Cathan so she could keep us safe in the sodding place we would die in. My eyes glanced over Faerie. Over the purple ground, the massive trees, all the way to the rocky cliffs that formed around the palace. *There are worse places to die,* I thought. Savannah rested her head on my shoulder and I smiled. *Yep. This place would bloody do for now.*

Though even with Savannah here, I didn't think I could ever be truly happy in Faerie. Cathan sure screwed us. What a bloody prat.

Chapter Three

Billie

*C*rystal Cauldron smelled like home, and as I walked through the tight space looking over the shelves lining the walls with the crystals and herbs, I couldn't help but smile. So many memories, so many secrets uncovered in this one little shop. So much uncovered about myself. As far as I was concerned, the Crystal Cauldron was where I became *me* again. And Ms. Broussard, who was nowhere to be found, was a motherly figure of sorts. It was funny to think that for the longest time I thought I didn't have a mother at all, yet as it turned out, I had quite a few.

River trailed behind me, careful not to knock anything over as he made his way through the narrow shop. I tried not to laugh because with his broad shoulders and stoic build, he was very much a bull in a China shop. I rushed to the front counter, placing my fingers on the glass, and rose on my tiptoes to look through the small back door leading to the shop owner's apartment.

"Ms. Broussard!" I yelled out. No answer. My eyes flashed to River, worry creasing my brow. "Ms. Broussard!"

Light steps hurried down the back hall and sent shivers down my spine. I let myself relax, dropping down on my heels again. Close call. I didn't know what anybody would want with the elderly shop owner. She had no magic. She wasn't a witch. She wasn't a shadower. She was a human who happened to run the only magic shop in Shadowhurst. She also happened to be the only human who knew about magic and lived to tell about it, so that made her pretty damn special in my books.

I ran my fingers through the crystal necklace display atop the counter and sucked in their energy with a sigh. It wasn't that long ago that I first came to the shop and Ms. Broussard gave me one of these for free. I thought it was simply her being nice to the new girl in town, but I was way off base. Ms. Broussard caught wind that I was a witch, and not just any witch, but the daughter of Beatrix Stonewall, someone she knew very well back in the day. Talk about a small world.

As the energy of the crystals settled deep inside my belly, I heard the rustling footsteps from down the hall near closer and straightened my back. Moments later, Ms. Broussard emerged through the doorway, silver hair braided loosely and eyes fierce and full of life. Her long, flowy skirt caught on the side of the door and she yanked it loose, the bangles running all the way up her forearm jingling.

I yanked my hand away from the crystals, hoping she didn't notice the mess I made of her display, and smiled.

The shop owner's eyes crinkled. "Billie! Lovely to see you again. I didn't expect you back so soon."

"We wanted to check if you found something." My cheeks reddened as I spoke, realizing she likely had no time to even look, since we were last here yesterday. *I am an actual idiot.*

"No, my dear," Ms. Broussard said. "But since you're here, I have some tea brewing if you're interested in joining me."

I could all but hear River bouncing from foot to foot behind me. "It sounds lovely."

As Ms. Broussard unlocked the tiny door on the counter and motioned for us to follow her, I shot River my most annoyed looking glare and elbowed him in the side. We didn't have time for tea, but I knew if I refused, I'd never hear the end of it.

River closed the door and hurried after me, nearly salivating as we got closer to Ms. Broussard's magical tea. I couldn't blame him. I loved spending time with the shop owner, and with everything that's happened lately, I hadn't had a chance to do it as often. *Maybe when all of this was over, I could make sure to visit more.* I was certain Ms. Broussard wouldn't mind. In fact, she told me many times to stop by and I never listened. Because there was always something that came up. Someone was always trying to kill us.

We made our way down the hallway, and I felt the energy shift as the runes protecting the shop owner's home took effect. For someone who wasn't a witch, Ms. Broussard sure had this place spelled to the brim. I eyed the etchings as she unlocked the door and let us inside, motioning to the couch in the living room.

River was nice and comfy on the couch before I could even get settled. I laughed. "You're such a nerd." He flashed his pearly whites, and that cute dimple on his cheek made an appearance. "You know that doesn't work if you already got the girl."

"Sure it does," he said. "You once told me that dimple could make you do anything I want."

I rolled my eyes. "Full of yourself much, hunter?"

I didn't know why I kept calling him that when River was more wolf than hunter these days, but I guess the nickname stuck. Besides, it reminded me of when we first met. A much simpler and much less confusing time—despite the fact that I was being hunted by him and his friends and hiding right under their noses.

Before I had a chance to get lost down memory lane, the sound of plates clanking against each other pulled me back to reality as I watched Ms. Broussard lower a tray of teas and other goodies onto the coffee table.

"I take it you've had no success at the portal site?" she asked.

I shook my head. "Not even a little. I don't understand why I can't get it open. Cathan did something no one can figure out, and I refuse to believe he's that much smarter than all of us."

"Trickier," Ms. Broussard corrected. "Not smarter."

I forced out a meek smile. "You really haven't been able to find anything in the books?"

The shop owner's face dropped, and I had my answer. She'd made about as much progress as the rest of us, it seemed. I reached for my tea, noticing River had already downed half of his. I was about to take a sip when my phone vibrated in my pocket.

"Hello?"

"It's me. Are you at the Crystal Cauldron?" Peyton shrieked on the other end.

"I am. What's up?"

"We think we found something!"

My eyes bulged and confusion laced my features. What could Peyton have possibly found at the portal site? We'd been over the witch graveyard with a fine-toothed comb and came up empty, and it wasn't like she had some hidden abilities as a shadower. Soul suckers—Peyton's kind of shadower —could do a whole lot of damage, but sniffing out clues wasn't on their list of special powers. That was more of a shifter thing.

"You there?" Peyton asked.

Crap. I must have zoned out again. "I am, yeah. Sorry. You said you found something?"

"Yep! Not sure what it means, but I figured if you're with Ms. Broussard you might as well ask her. She is a walking encyclopedia, after all."

I didn't like putting the shop owner in a situation where she couldn't say no, so I said, "I could call Sebyl if you want."

"No, we have no time for her attitude right now."

I stifled a giggle. "Okay, hold on, I'll put you on speaker." I pressed a button and put the phone on the coffee table, sliding it closer to Ms. Broussard.

"Am I good to go?" Peyton screamed.

"You are, and you know, take it down a notch. We can hear you fine." River stiffened at my side, but I brushed him off; I knew my best friend could take the attitude. She had quite a bit of it on her own.

"Okay, so here's the thing. Morgan and I stayed back to see if we can discover something over at the site, and we got nowhere."

My mouth dropped open. "I thought you said you found something."

"Girl, let me finish. So, there was nothing and Morgan said she had to, well, you know... we had a few grande iced coffees in the morning and then she decided to have another coffee after that. 'Nuf said, yeah? Anyway, she went off to do her business, then, like a second later, comes running back screaming my name. I thought something happened and rushed over there, but she was fine."

"Can you get to the part of you finding something?" I asked, cutting her off. Peyton's stories could go on for a while, and I doubted Miss Broussard had the time or the patience to listen to her blabber on about Morgan's bathroom break.

"Right. Yeah, sorry. Where was I? Oh, yes! Right where she was about to go, this weird dust covered the ground."

"Dust?" River asked, one eyebrow quirking.

"Yeah, that's what I said. I didn't think anything of it, but Morgan said it looked like it didn't quite fit in."

I frowned and got closer to the phone. "Could they be doing some construction at the cemetery?"

"What? Are you listening? There was no construction. It looked weird. Trust me. We scooped up the hella strange dust and brought it to the resistance house. You'll never guess what it was! Ground up garnet!"

"Ground garnet," Ms. Broussard repeated in a whisper to no one in particular.

I trained my gaze on her. "Does that mean something?"

Ms. Broussard lifted a finger and shuffled out of the room. We didn't have to wait long before the shop owner came rushing back with an ancient book in her hands. She flipped the pages, grazing each one with her fingers as she read. "There," she said, pointing to one page in particular. "There it is."

Cold sweat licked at my neck as I took the book from her and turned it around to read. "Crushed garnet, three raw amethysts, seven drops of fae blood, beach wood essence." My eyes narrowed the last ingredient. If it required beach wood, chances were dark magic was involved. This was not good.

"Okay, sounds suspicious," Peyton said, reading my mind. "What does it make?"

I scanned the pages. "Oh, crap."

"What?" everyone exclaimed simultaneously. Everyone except Ms. Broussard, who I assumed already knew the world of garbage we were about to walk into.

Squaring my jaw, I said, "It's a magical bomb of some kind."

"Let me see that," River said and yanked the book from my hands. "Yep. She's right, it's a bomb. And not any bomb. It says here if created correctly, this bomb can be made to target anyone who has magic. No matter where they are."

"How the hell is that possible? How did we not know this thing existed?"

Ms. Broussard's nose wrinkled, and she straightened her shoulders. "I would think it is because no one thought the fae were still alive."

My stomach turned and tears started to collect behind my eyes, blurring my vision. Was this what Cathan had in mind? Is that why he made sure we couldn't get the portal open so that none of his precious fae would get hurt when the bomb went off? Or was it to prevent any of us from escaping? I knew he was a bastard, but this was going to be a massacre. An execution of every creature on Earth who had magic. If Cathan created this bomb, wouldn't it kill him too? I shook the question off—knowing my damn father, he had some protections to guarantee his own safety. My lunch tried to come back up and I swallowed the acidic taste, flipping through the book's pages. "Is there anything here that says how to stop it?"

"I can look into it," Ms. Broussard said, "but in order to stop it, you'd have to find the bomb first. I don't suppose your friend found it while she was taking care of business?"

Peyton stifled a giggle on the other end of the line. "Nope. All we got was the dust and we're lucky even found that. Everyone, thank Morgan's tiny bladder!"

This was a disaster. *We are so freaking screwed.*

I must have said that part out loud because Ms. Broussard whispered, "Oh, you're a lot worse than that."

I looked at her, baffled. "How could it be worse?"

"This isn't simply a bomb. Once created, a timer is activated to guarantee the correct functioning of the weapon."

River groaned beside me. "How much time do we have?"

For a moment, everyone grew silent. When Ms. Broussard finally spoke, my entire world crashed into a million pieces.

"Around 72 hours, give or take."

Holy crap. We had three days to save the entire magical community. No pressure at all.

Chapter Four

River

amn that bastard! I truly wished Billie had let me kill Cathan when I had the chance, because now he made sure none of us were getting out alive. I couldn't believe a creature that vile created someone as amazing as Billie. I kept my thoughts to myself, hoping to spare my mate from any more unnecessary turmoil. The ride from to the resistance house had Billie up in knots, and I knew she was anxious even without checking our mate marks. She already took on too much—let people depend on her—and now she had three days to save those people. *I'm going to kill that prick when I get my hands on him.*

I laughed at myself. How exactly was I going to kill a man made entirely of shadow? All talk and no bite was not a great look for an alpha wolf.

Deep inside, the beast tore at my soul. He too knew the dangers we were facing, and he wanted to rip Cathan apart, same as I did.

"We'll figure it out," Billie said. Her voice drew me back

to reality, and I realized I was white-knuckling the wheel. "Right?"

I nodded, afraid to speak in case she could hear the lies in my voice. I had no fucking clue if we would figure anything out this time. I pulled the car into the small parking lot in the woods, uncurled my spine, and put on the best happy face I could muster. "Come on. Everyone should be there already. I'm sure someone will come up with a good idea."

Literally no one had an idea. My fists shook under the table as I sat as still as humanly possible, grinding my teeth. I willed my brain to work, but came up empty, much like everyone else in the musty old room. It wasn't a small group either. Aside from the two of us at the round table in the house, sat Lorelei, Raiden, Mel, Peyton, and Morgan. Lorelei, the mind reaper representative of the shadower resistance, appeared extra ethereal today. Her platinum hair, braided into intricate designs at the crown of her head, looked like it took hours to do. She flicked her violet eyes my way and I looked at my feet, embarrassed she caught me staring. But could you blame me? She looked completely out of place next to Raiden and Mel, the two shifter leaders. Then again, Mel's leave-nothing-to-the-imagination leather outfit and Raiden's seven-foot frame didn't exactly blend in either.

Directly behind Raiden, huddled against a wall, stood Beatrix and Catarina with a couple rogue witches I hadn't met yet. I was surprised the high priestesses didn't bother showing up, but I supposed Beatrix was here to pass over any pertinent information back to the High Coven. It was a head trip to see Billie's mom representing the High Coven, but that was a thought for another time.

I looked around the room. The mind reaper, shifters, and soul sucker represented the shadower resistance as a whole. Between Beatrix and Catarina, we had the witches covered. Billie made up for the fae, or at least the half of her that was fae did. This place was like a circus car full of paranormals, though I supposed when you dealt with the big bad, everyone's opinion mattered. Especially when their lives were at stake.

In the end, it mattered little who was here. No one had the slightest inkling of where we could even begin to search for the damn bomb.

"We know it must be somewhere at the portal site," Peyton said.

The red streaks in her hair were brighter today, like blood stains against the black of her pin-straight hair. She wore a studded motorcycle jacket and a jumpsuit that I could only describe as prison-chic. Beside her, Morgan was a complete opposite. Flowery dress all the way to her toes, fiery red hair down her back, and a diamond-crusted choker across her neck. I had no idea how these two were an item, but I guessed it was true what they said, opposites attracted.

"Not necessarily," Beatrix countered. "Cathan could've easily created the bomb at the cemetery and transferred it elsewhere for safekeeping."

"That tracks," Morgan said. "It would be foolish for him to hide the stupid thing in the cemetery where he knew we'd check."

"It was foolish of him to leave that powder behind," I said.

Billie, who had been silent this entire meeting, rose a

little off her chair. She leaned her elbows on the table and placed her chin in the crook of her open palms. "He wanted us to find it."

"What? Why?" I asked. "Maybe he missed it by mistake."

"Cathan doesn't make mistakes. No, this was intentional. He knew we'd find the powder sooner or later. He knew we'd figure out what it was. And he knew we wouldn't know how to stop it. This was planned."

"He didn't know you were going to trap him in his shadow form, did he?"

Billie sighed and leaned back in her chair. Her blue eyes darkened and I felt her turmoil through our bond. "No," she answered. "That he did not know, which is what makes this entire situation even worse. Cathan made sure the bomb was set to go off. Since there's a timer that functions alongside the magic, I'm certain he assumed he'd be around to stop it in case something went wrong. He wouldn't dare put his precious fae in danger."

"*Your* precious fae," I corrected.

"Right."

"What about some sort of a protection spell?" Beatrix asked. "I think Luna was working on one that was big enough to cover an entire city block."

It was freaking weird hearing Billie's mom speak of the high priestess as though they were old friends. Almost as though this wasn't the same witch that had her imprisoned for the last decade. Really freaking weird.

"We could try to implement it once we find the bomb," Billie said.

That was the part that was going to prove to be the most difficult. If I knew anything about Cathan, it was that he was a secretive bastard. If this prick wanted to hide something, it would sure as hell stay hidden. He hid in plain sight, and no one even knew it was him until it was too late. My heart twisted thinking about that bastard wearing my mother's face like some sort of skin suit. Cathan managed to fool all of us into thinking he was her after the prison break Billie pulled off to get Beatrix out of the magical jail cell the coven kept her in, all to get close to us. I'm not sure how we missed it. I should have known Mom was dead the second I laid eyes on her likeness, and yet I didn't. I was blind to Cathan's tricks like everyone else. I hated that I didn't know it wasn't her. I hated that she died all alone. And I hated myself for being somewhat relieved that she was gone. Our relationship was always complicated, but it became even more so after she killed all those students to drain their magic. At least with her gone I didn't have to deal with the fact that I still loved her, even though she was such a colossal monster.

"Babe? Babe?"

I bristled. "Sorry. What did you say?"

"I said, do you think some of the wolves could hit the graveyard later today? See if they can sniff out something else. Perhaps there's another clue they can uncover, now that we know what we're looking for."

"Sure, I'll ask." My eyes met Raiden's and he held my gaze, telling me exactly what I already knew—they would find nothing. Billie was right. Cathan planted the powder for us to find, and unless he planted another clue, there would be nothing left to sniff out. I looked around the table and the people gathered here and my insides burned. What I wouldn't give to protect each one of them. My gaze landed on Billie—I would protect her the most. "I have an idea you're not going to like," I said. Everyone's expectant faces turned to me as I swallowed the pool of saliva gathering under my tongue. "We could just ask him."

"No! *Hell* no!" Peyton yelled. "There is no way we are going to free that asshole from the shadow prison he's in! Right, Billie?"

My mate shot me an apologetic look and looked down at her hands. "No, we will not. Freeing Cathan is not an option. We'll figure this out on our own. Let's call your idea Plan B."

I knew exactly what she meant by Plan B—it meant "never happening, buddy."

"Come on! We have to give it a try. We have only three days, and I think we can all agree that the chances of us figuring this out on our own are slim to none. I'm not implying that I'm not worried the asshole will go crazy once we free him and try to escape, but we can handle this. We can have backup in place to make sure it doesn't happen."

"Cathan is as slippery as they come," Beatrix said. "I should know. If you think you'll be able to trap him again now that he knows how you did it in the first place, you're insane."

"Mom..."

"I'm only saying what we're all thinking. I know you mean well, River, and I know you want to protect my daughter, but that cannot be the way we do it."

I rose to stand, pushing away from the table. Billie's soft palm pressed to my forearm as I gritted my teeth. "Babe, don't go."

"*I need some air,*" I said through our bond.

Turning from the table, I hissed out a quick '*I'm sorry*' and headed for the door. As they continued to bounce ideas off each other that I knew would lead to more dead ends, I slammed the door behind me. My shoulders hunched as I stalked through the house, making my way to the back porch. I needed to be free. I needed to run. Inside me, the wolf whimpered, and I all but tore through the rear of the house. I hit the ground on all fours, my back straining and my skin stretching, the wolf emerging from within. My warm breath rose before me in the chilled afternoon air, and I pointed my snout to the sky, letting out a howl. As I got ready to run, a low growl sounded behind me and I turned on my heel. My eyes met the golden gaze of a lion and my wolf relaxed. Raiden's lion stood tall in the small clearing behind the resistance house, blocking out the sun above us. He pointed his large, wet nose to the woods. I lowered my head in agreement.

As we took off, our talons leaving deep gashes in the Earth behind us, my mind and body relaxed. I didn't agree with the others and I still thought freeing Cathan was the best plan, but I also wasn't so proud I couldn't see their point. I would give Billie time to figure this out, but if they failed, I would find a way to free Cathan myself. And I would make that prick bleed and pray for death when I was done with him.

Cathan thought he won, but he was a fool if he thought I would sit down and watch while he destroyed everyone I loved. He would not win again. I had to make sure of it. No matter what Billie and the rest of them wanted, I was an alpha. And an alpha protected his pack by any means necessary.

Chapter Five

Billie

*R*iver was acting like a Grade A jerk, but he was my jerk, so I knew I had to give him his space. As difficult as it was not to yell at him in front of everyone for being so damn stubborn, I knew that he only needed to vent and he'd be back to normal, and chose the higher ground. I mean, one of us had to be the bigger person, right? Since I was usually the one to hold a grudge, I figured this time that person could be me. Besides, having a run with Raiden would do him a lot more good than having it out with me.

Which is exactly why, when the meeting that led nowhere finished, I headed back to the Chandlers' to get some much-needed rest. The house smelled of blueberry muffins as soon as I walked in, and my mouth salivated thinking about what sweet concoction Thomas had created this time. I heard laughter in the dining room, tossed my shoes off, and hurried in, hoping I hadn't missed out on the deliciousness.

As I all but skidded into the dining room, Imala and

Thomas looked up from the table and offered me the warmest of smiles. I always felt so welcome here. To make the couple even better candidates for the Humans of the Year award, they had been amazing since Beatrix started coming around the house. When it came to Shadowhurst, I could not imagine a life without the Chandlers in it.

I knew they weren't my parents, but they sure felt like family.

Footsteps shuffled behind me, and I swung around to see Alfred carrying a tray of iced lattes into the room. Three in total, like he knew ahead of time I would be here. No shock there, Alfred knew everything. If it wasn't for his horrible run-in with a shifter and the shock on his face thereafter, I would have been convinced he had magic.

"Welcome back, Miss Stonewall," Alfred said, his thick accent rising to the surface.

I snatched one of the iced lattes. "Thanks, Alfred. It's good to be back."

"We were wondering if you had moved out," Thomas joked.

I laughed sheepishly. "I had a lot going on with River." Imala crooked her brows and I quickly added, "But also Peyton and my mom. I hope it's okay that she's been coming around?"

"Oh, are you kidding? We're glad she's here! It must be nice to have her back after all these years. To be honest, after what your caseworker said, we were expecting the worst, but I don't see it. She seems perfectly wonderful to me."

I almost choked on my iced latte. My caseworkers in this case were the high priestesses, and I cringed thinking about the first visit they made the Chandlers' home. How they managed to convince anyone they were social workers was beyond me; the women stank of magic. Though the Chandlers didn't really know magic existed, which explained why they fell for the high priestesses' act so easily. Great for me, since I got to live in the most lavish house I'd ever stepped foot in. Between the Chandlers and my mom, it felt like I was having my cake and eating it, too.

Then there was Cathan.

My heart stopped for a second.

I reached over the table to snatch two muffins from the plate. "Mind if I take this over to the guest house?" I asked. "I have a bit of homework to catch up on."

"Of course," Thomas said with a smile. I was already on my feet when he asked, "Will you be around for dinner?"

"I sure will!" I yelled over my shoulder, clutched my latte and bolted to the back of the house. Even after all this time, I wasn't used to the opulence of the Chandler residence. It truly was a masterpiece—modern and spacious and airy, every detail chosen as carefully as a centerpiece. With a smell of fresh muffins wafting through my nose, I ran down the backyard, opened the door to the guest house, and plunked myself on the small sofa in the center of the living room. Because yes, I had a living room. I still couldn't believe it.

Shame coursed through me when I thought about the lie I told. There was no homework. In fact, I'd missed so many classes, I wasn't sure I'd be able to graduate this year. Peyton said she cleared my absence with some of the teachers and I could make up for it during summer school. I didn't have the heart to tell her what I thought of the idea—that I wasn't certain I, or any of us, would be alive by summer. Needless to say, my positivity had all but evaporated since we reached yet another dead end at the meeting.

I pushed the school out of my mind and fought to keep my eyes open. Somehow, sitting down brought on all the exhaustion I had stuffed away, covering me in waves of sleepiness. The thought of making it to the bedroom seemed excruciating and before I knew it, the guest house went completely dark.

My eyes flashed open in a panic. The air in the guest-house was suffocating, as though there wasn't quite enough of it. I looked around, groggy from sleep, my fingers clutching the couch, and panic laced through me. I couldn't feel the couch fabric under me. Instead, something wet and slimy slid between my fingers.

Groaning, I peered down at the bright shade of purple all around my body. *No,* I thought. *This can be happening.* My eyes focused as I ogled the land before me, a sight I didn't think I'd see again. *Faerie? How am I in Faerie?*

I hopped up and dusted myself off.

This has to be a dream. There's no other way to explain it.

Slowly, I picked up a steady pace and walked until I reached a large copse of trees in the distance. They were bigger than I remembered, but I couldn't expect my dreams to be a replica of the place. My breath came short, and I ran my finger over the bark of one tree. It felt so real...

As I skirted around the tree trunks, a smile tugged at my lips, and I let myself get absorbed into memory. As dangerous as our adventure in the realm was, I really did miss it. It was so beautiful. And having all that magic around me, being able to use fae energy so freely was an experience unlike any other. I really hoped that we could save Earth's paranormals so I could visit again someday. Leaves rustled behind me as I spun around to see nothing but forest. My palms were slicked with sweat as I called for my shadow magic, quickly realizing that a dream could not pose any real danger, and even if it could, the chances of me being able to use my magic in a dream state were slim to none. I dug my heels into the ground, my eyes widening as several branches parted in the distance and a tall figure stepped out to meet me. The young man's shoulders were broad, and his muscular physique jetted out solidly against the plush background of dream Faerie. Deep hazel eyes zeroed in on me, and I took a step back, flustered.

"Can I help you?" I asked. *Why are you even asking? This is* your *dream. Don't be an idiot.*

"Billie Stonewall, I presume?" the man asked. Now that he inched closer to me, it became quite obvious that he was fae. Everything about him was inhuman and perfect, from his short, thick hair to the bulging muscles of his arms, straight down to the fae outfit he was wearing—which in this case, didn't cover all that much. I tried not to blush as I glanced at the water droplets on his torso.

A water fae, I thought. The idea bewildered me. There weren't many water fae left, and from what I remembered, most of them were female. A male water fae—how odd.

"Not that odd," the man responded.

Ugh, did I say that out loud?

"You don't have to say anything out loud. I can hear what you're thinking."

Awkward. "Right, it's my dream." I let out a long sigh. "Why did I conjure you, of all people?"

The fae laughed. He straight up keeled over his thighs and laughed at me. Turned out that even my dreams thought I was a joke. Great.

While the annoying water fae collected himself, I took note of the odd drawings on his arms. I couldn't quite make out what they were, but they seemed to be written in an ancient language, covering every inch of his skin all the way to his shoulders.

"You didn't conjure me, Billie," he finally said. "I'm actually here."

"I don't understand. What do you mean, you're here?"

"In your dream, Billie." He reached out a hand, but dropped it to his side when I didn't take it. Shaking his head, he said, "My name is Solen. It's nice to meet you. Victoria told me you'd be skeptical, so I apologize if this is difficult to wrap your head around."

"You know Vic?" I had many questions.

"Yes, I do."

Well, that answered pretty much nothing. I crossed my arms and tried not to let my face show the frustration I felt. The fae were notorious for skirting around the truth, and it was tedious to drag information out of them. At first I thought it was only Cathan, because he was such a lying monster, but nope! Every single fae acted like each piece of knowledge they held was a national treasure to be guarded. It was exasperating.

I looked Solen up and down. "How is any of this possible?"

"As you were thinking, there aren't that many male water fae in the realm, and the few that exist have a special ability that the females do not possess."

Realization dawned on me, and I stifled my disbelief long enough to say, "You're a Dream-walker."

"Correct."

"And Vic sent you into my dream. Is everything all right? Logan and Savannah?

"They're fine." Solen held up a hand to calm me. "Everybody is fine. With the portal closing so rapidly, Victoria wanted to know what happened. We had assumed the worst, so it's good to see you alive and well."

I ran my fingers through my hair. "I'm alive, but I'm not well," I told Solen. "We have a big, time-sensitive problem."

"According to Victoria, when it comes to Earth witches, there is always some sort of problem."

I laughed. "She's not wrong, except this time, the witches aren't the issue."

"I take it the ex-king didn't leave Faerie empty-handed," Solen whispered.

"No, no, he did not. We have quite a bit of a mess to handle back on Earth, and one that's going to affect every supernatural creature living there. Cathan planted some sort of magical bomb. We don't know where to find it, and in seventy-two hours it's going to destroy everyone who has magic on Earth."

"That would explain the portal closing," Solen said.

"What do you mean?"

The fae parted his full lips, then closed them shut. He did this several times, as though he were chewing on invisible gum while he tried to choose his next words carefully. I wondered if Vic had perhaps painted me in a bad light and he was worried my short fuse would catch fire if he said the wrong thing. "Cathan was always convinced the fae race was superior to all other magical creatures. It makes sense that he would want to destroy all other beings that he deemed less palpable to his tastes. In doing so, he would need to make sure the fae are protected, so that they may flourish when the deed is done."

"I thought that might be the case. But we have no idea how to find the bomb or how to stop it when we do." My eyes narrowed on his. "Do you think you and the others can work on it on your end? Maybe there's something that you can find in Faerie, some clues Cathan left behind."

"I doubt the ex-king left clues, but we will try."

"Oh, and Solen?" I said. "We're kind of pressed for time here. How about we meet again in twenty-four hours? That should be enough time for you to look around."

Solen smiled and tilted his head down. "I'll make sure the others know time is of the essence."

"Thank you," I said.

This time, it was my hand reaching out to shake his. Solen's grip was strong, and I wondered how it was Vic knew the water fae. *Leave it to Vic to find one of the few hot water fae males and befriend him... Unless they're more than friends...*

"I can still hear everything you're thinking," Solen said, and my cheeks burned red.

He waved me off and turned to walk away, not bothering to say goodbye.

"Thank you again!" I yelled out to him, but it was too late. Faerie shimmered before me and dispersed, leaving only darkness behind. I shut my eyes tightly and when I opened them again, I was looking at the large television in the guest house, my own reflection staring back at me on the blank screen. My head pounded, and I reached to rub at my temples, my gaze catching sight of my fingernails. My very *purple* fingernails. Somehow I carried a piece of dream Faerie back with me. I wasn't sure how it happened, and made a mental note to ask Sebyl if it's something the High Coven has heard of before—a dream coming to life.

Groggily, I pulled out my cell phone and dialed Peyton.

"We need to meet up," I said when she answered. "Get everyone you can find."

"Is everything okay?"

"Better than okay," I answered, grinning. "I think I just witnessed a miracle."

Chapter
Six

Savannah

*T*he sun hid behind the clouds, cooling the puddle of sweat collecting at the base of my back as we made our way through the dense forest of Faerie. Behind us, the cliffs rose in the distance, hiding the palace from view. Despite the urgency of our mission here, it was a relief to get out of the palace for a change. Ever since the portal closed, it was awful lonely here; friends were hard to come by. Whatever false picture Cathan painted of a realm where everyone works together was a big fat lie. Faerie was one massive gladiator ring: everyone for themselves and always ready to fight. Usually I didn't have trouble making friends, though I think that had to do more with my particular shade of friendship—one that was more akin to control and one I no longer employed. It wasn't that long ago that I was the most popular girl in Shadowhurst Academy. It was bliss, sort of. The problem with being the Queen B—as Peyton called me behind my back—was keeping up appearances. I had to be the best at everything. Unfortunately for everyone around me, to be the best meant I had to take others down. Peyton was right, I was a bitch with a capital B. That was until I met Logan. No matter how much I tried to push him away, he pushed right back. Logan got me; he understood why I was so hard on everyone all the time. Why I was so hard on myself. Maybe it was that understanding that softened me up around the edges. Gross.

I looked around, and my heart sank at the memory of Shadowhurst and everyone we left behind when we stayed in Faerie. I missed them. I even missed Billie, and I freaking hated to admit it.

"Are we almost there?" I asked for the millionth time. A few steps in front of me, Logan's shoulders tightened, his silver hair swaying slightly. I wondered if he was sick of hearing it.

Whatever. I didn't care. We'd been walking for an hour and I didn't even know what we were walking toward. Ever since Solen returned with some miraculous message from Billie—the nature of which I didn't quite understand—Logan had been on a mission to question every damn fae in the realm. No one knew anything about a magical bomb. Big surprise there. I felt like a tool with the first fae we asked, and by the time we got to the twentieth, well, let's say I was done. I was also hungry as hell. Not a great combination.

We rounded a small lake and I kicked a pebble into the water as we passed. Dark shadows formed beneath the surface and guilt tightened in my abdomen. *Good job, girl. You stoned someone's house.*

There was so much in Faerie to get used to, though I didn't think I'd ever get the hang of the water fae—they were too different. I glanced behind me at Vic and Solen, deep in conversation. *Guess the witch doesn't have the same problem.*

"Remind me why we need to walk this far out to speak with the Earth fae?" I asked Logan. His annoyed expression and narrowed violet eyes made my teeth grind together to stop from telling him off. Instead of choosing the petty route, I smiled and said, "You're the king, Logan. If you need to talk to someone, they will come to you."

"I'm not going to make people go out of their way to speak with me when I can very well walk to meet them. I have legs for a reason, all four of us do."

"Do we though?" I hissed between clenched teeth and looked at Solen again. He sure had some long legs now, but I wasn't so sure what the boy had going on in the water. Shaking myself into alertness, I ran to catch up to Logan. "Billie said we only had, what? Seventy-two hours until this thing goes off? And she gave us a day to find information. Do we really have time to be traipsing around questioning people who are clueless?"

"It's worth a try, isn't it, love? Unless you have another idea on how we can find the information Billie asked for?"

I looked down at my feet and kept walking. I wasn't sure there was information here for Billie. If the High Coven didn't have a clue, what were the chances we would? I mean, I only found out about magic recently, and Logan didn't even know he was fae until a month before we ended up in this realm. When it came to magical knowledge, our best source was Victoria, and she seemed more preoccupied with Solen these days. I tried not to turn around for fear of catching the two in a compromising position. The witch denied any kind of relationship between them, but my gut told me otherwise. If there's anything I knew, it was how to smell out couples when I saw them. I wasn't the matchmaker of Shadowhurst Academy for nothing! I cringed, thinking about Shadowhurst and my silly little crush on River for all those years. Maybe I wasn't as good a matchmaker as I thought. Memories of Shadowhurst flooded my mind, and I quickly erected mental walls before I wandered down memory lane.

Head in the game, lady. Save Shadowhurst, then reminisce.

I rolled my shoulders and straightened my back. Looping my fingers through Logan's, I trained my eyes on the horizon and said, "Let's see if this is our lucky break."

"That was a complete dud," I ground out, as we made the long journey back to the palace, returning empty-handed once again.

"Not entirely. At least now we know the Earth fae are as daft as the rest," Logan said.

I had no idea how he was making light of the situation. We had eighteen hours to go before Solen was to meet Billie in... something about dream walking. Whatever, I wasn't listening. The point was that time was of the essence, and Logan was making little jokes like we were on a freaking cruise over here.

"Something on your mind, love?"

"I don't understand how you could take this so lightly."

Logan's expression darkened, and he looked ahead with determination. "What else would you have me do?"

"I don't know, maybe act like this is serious?" I scoffed.

"I know this is serious and I know you think we're faffing around," he said. "I'm trying to stay positive about the situation. One of us needs to keep a level head."

"Excuse me?" I stopped in my tracks, hands flying to my

waist instantly. "I will have you know, Reaper, my head is on quite level. Everyone agrees that we are pretty much screwed. There is not one fae in the realm that has had an inkling of knowledge of a magical bomb, and it's not like Cathan would up and tell his little plan to anyone, but—"

"The fire fae," we said in unison.

Logan's eyes burned. "If Cathan spilled his guts to anyone, it was his minging guards."

Too bad his guards were either dead or escaped into Shadowhurst. "Do you think Billie could track them down?" I asked.

"If anyone could track the fae, it's my sister."

"Let's hope she hasn't killed them yet." I laughed to ease the tension, because we both knew there was a good chance Billie might have unleashed her shadow wrath on those morons as soon as she got back home. I looked over my shoulder. "Any ideas on what we can do next, you two?"

Victoria and Solen barely acknowledged my existence. They shook their heads simultaneously and went back to whatever whispered conversation they were having.

"I think when they have an idea, they'll let you know," Logan said.

"What is up with them, anyway?"

He shrugged, and my excitement for gossip deflated instantly. Logan was good for many things, but hot gossip was not one of them. Man, did I miss Morgan! That girl had the nose of a bloodhound when it came to information. She even knew where I left my favorite bracelet in Grade 3, after I spent days looking for it. Turned out it was right under my nose the entire... "Wait!" I yelled out and everyone stopped dead in their tracks. "What if the bomb isn't on Earth at all?"

Solen crooked an eyebrow while Logan and Victoria stared at me like I was one marble short of a full set.

"What if it's here?" I said. "In Faerie."

"Why would Cathan plant a bomb in the one place he wanted to protect?" Logan asked.

"I don't know. To make sure no one on Earth could get to it?"

"That doesn't make sense," Victoria spoke. *Thanks for your two cents. Ugh.* "If the bomb goes off in Faerie, it'll destroy every fae, and the running theory we have is that it is meant for the supernaturals back on Earth. I don't think Cathan plans to kill the entire fae race."

I was about to tell her to shove it when I noticed Logan speed up ahead. "Why are you rushing?"

He barely slowed to answer. "You might be onto something here," he said. "The bomb is likely not in Faerie, though perhaps the trigger is. If there is a safety in place, it would fare better for Cathan to plant it somewhere Billie could not easily get to."

He waved his arm around aimlessly.

"You think he left a way to stop it somewhere in this realm."

"It's a possibility."

The knots in my neck tightened, and I felt the start of a headache rapidly approaching. The more I thought about Cathan's plan, the less it made sense. He must have known we'd come to this conclusion, and it seemed as though the idiot was playing the worst game of hide-and-seek ever. Everyone knew if you wanted to hide something, you didn't make it easy access. Even if there was a fail-safe somewhere in Faerie, he must have known Billie would try to open the portal to retrieve it. Something didn't add up, and it was making me furious not to know what it was. My eyes knifed to Logan's retreating back as I rushed to keep up. "You're running like someone who knows where he's going."

"We'd been going around this wrong," Logan said. "We assumed Cathan would leave a clue with the fae, but the twat was much too secretive to share his plans. There was only one person Cathan trusted enough to hold his secrets."

"Cathan," I whispered. "You think there's something hidden in the palace."

"In the library. I think Cathan may have left himself the magical version of a Post-it note. I don't believe he expected to leave so swiftly, so we might get lucky."

It was a stretch, but it sure beat walking aimlessly around Faerie for the rest of the day, so I nodded and hurried along with him. The sun burned the rear of my neck, and I swatted at the wet spots with my hand, not breaking stride with Logan. Behind us, Victoria and Solen's footsteps slowed until I couldn't hear them, and I didn't need to turn around to know the two had vanished to do who knows what. They pulled the disappearing act so often one would think they had a magic act in Vegas to practice for.

"They'll come around when they need to," Logan said, sensing my annoyance.

I nodded.

My posture stiffened, and I pumped my legs, nearly running now. If I knew anything about the fae, or at least the fae that was Logan's father, it's that he was a tricky bastard. Whether the bomb was on Earth or in Faerie, whether there was a fail-safe or not, either way, it was definitely not going to be where we would expect. That sneaky little pig hid it somewhere he thought no one would find it, and I was going to prove him wrong. I wondered how Cathan would feel about a human outsmarting him. With that thought at the forefront of my mind, I closed the distance between myself and the palace. *We're going to figure this out, Cathan. This is not how it ends for us.*

Chapter Seven

Billie

"*I* believe your wolf might have a point."

Darkness swarmed my vision and my skin burned. I leveled myself to gape at Sebyl in disbelief. "What did you say?"

The high priestess didn't even bat an eyelash at my horror. Her sharp bangs cut across her face and though her brows were hidden, I was pretty sure they rested in the same better-than-thou expression they always had. "Your boyfriend is on to something," she repeated. "Freeing Cathan from his hold may be our best solution."

I seriously couldn't believe what I was hearing. No. I refused to believe it. Of all people, I would think Sebyl would be the last one to want Cathan freed, not after everything she did to make sure her coven knew nothing of the fae. My back curled, and I hunched in on myself like a rag doll with its center stuffing removed.

"Like my mom said," I reminded them, "once he's out, he won't let us trap him again."

"I am well aware of Cathan's prowess. However, as your

boyfriend pointed out, we really are running out of options. I have witches working around the clock looking for the bomb's location, and they are yet to come back with anything concrete. And as I'm sure you're well aware of, if the High Coven can't figure this out, no one can."

Well, at least we knew Sebyl was still Sebyl. The self-assuredness of this woman was uncanny. I would have thought that after working with Catarina and the rogues, she would be open to the possibility that others might know what they're doing. But no, as always, the high priestess did as the high priestess wanted, and what she wanted, what she always wanted, was to be in control of everything around her. That meant *she* had to be the best. No one else.

I looked around the room. It was surreal to be back in the townhouse. It's been so long since I stepped foot through these doors—or been invited in. Spending time here for the last few weeks has been absolutely mind-boggling. It wasn't that I missed this place, not by a long shot. In fact, as I sat in the High Coven dining room with my fingers digging holes into the large oak table, the last thing I wanted was to live under Sebyl's roof again. When Beatrix first told me she planned to move in, I pretty much blew a fuse. We went through hell to free her from the prison these witches put her in, and here she was, running right back like nothing happened. I was convinced my mother had a pretty serious case of Stockholm syndrome, but after a few days, I realized she was right. The only way to keep an eye on the High Coven was to literally keep an eye on them. So we agreed it was best for Beatrix to take advantage of the vast research facility that the High Coven had to offer, while also making sure they stayed in line and didn't go off on some solo mission to take control, as Sebyl often did.

"What about the portal?" Rhiamon asked.

"What about it?" Sebyl hissed out in return. I was surprised to hear the harsh tone of voice she kept for me used toward a fellow high priestess.

Rhiamon, solid and stoic, did not seem to mind. Her eyes remained calm as she said, "We are working under the assumption that Cathan destroyed the portal to keep the fae safe from the explosion."

Sebyl and I nodded.

"If that is the case and the fae should happen to cross over to Earth, the former king would have no choice but to stop the explosion from happening."

The high priestess narrowed her dark-lined eyes and brushed her bangs down. "Now, Rhiamon, I do believe you make a very good point."

My head spun, and I cleared my bone-dry throat before speaking so I didn't barf all over the antique table. "Your plan is to open the portal miraculously, drag the fae across—likely against their will—free Cathan, and hope he actually stops the bomb from going off, then imprison him in his shadow-self yet again. Oh, and get the fae back over to Faerie so that the magic on Earth continues to exist. You do hear how impossible that sounds, right?" By the looks on their faces, I'd say the two high priestesses truly thought they could pull this off. When they didn't say a word, I continued. "Not only have we not found the bomb yet, but I'm not sure if you recall that I cannot open the portal without Logan."

"You really think your half-breed brother is the answer?" Sebyl asked, scoffing.

That's it! I'm going to kill her. I had to cross my legs and sit on my hands to keep from charging her. Rhiamon must have sensed my anger. She stood up from the table and gave

Sebyl a stern look. "Thus far, the two working together opened the portal. It's safe to assume that we either need Logan or an alternate conduit to aid Billie."

Eyes still narrowed, Sebyl tapped a dark-purple lacquered nail on the tabletop and glared at a spot on the wall beyond Rhiamon's head. Her perfectly pressed purple suit seemed to wrinkle before my eyes as the anger she tried to control bubbled to the surface. *Way to go, Rhiamon!*

When Sebyl remained silent, I sucked in a sharp breath and attempted a peace-offering smile. "Okay. Let's say you find a conduit and we manage to open the portal; do you have any plans on how you're going to keep Cathan under control?"

"I'm certain we can figure it out when the time comes," Sebyl said.

"You'll need to figure it out beforehand if you have any hope of getting one up on Cathan," I shot back. "Is there anything we can use to transfer his energy to another container when we're done with him? There must be a spell in the coven's grimoires to help us with this."

Sebyl's eyes burned into me. "We don't transfer energy," she bit out. "The coven's rules forbid it."

What? This was news to me. I knew the High Coven had a lot of rules in place, most for their own protection, but I'd never heard of anything being forbidden before. My lips thinned as I stared her down. "You're telling me there isn't a witch alive who tried an energy transfer spell before?"

"There was one..." Sebyl's words trailed off. "No matter. All you need to know, child, is energy transfer spells are a dark, dangerous magic and they will not help you here."

I rolled my eyes so hard they nearly got stuck in the back of my head. Before I could give her a piece of my mind, the dining room door burst open and a frazzled-looking Luna came rushing through. The silver chains adorning her forehead swayed as she ran, and the smell of patchouli that often followed her wafted into the room. Fast on her heels, my mother walked in looking as concerned.

"You all need to come with us," Luna exclaimed, her violet eyes wide.

Next to me, Sebyl rustled in her seat and exchanged a look with Rhiamon that I couldn't quite read. If I was to guess, the two were on the outs with Luna, but I had no clue why. Out of the four high priestesses, Luna was the only one not prone to drama and competition. As long as I've known the witch, she had kept to herself, too busy reading the signs of the universe and studying to mind the petty business the other three concerned themselves with. Come to think of it, since moving back in, it was Luna who stayed by my mother's side. I almost thought they might have become friends again.

Perhaps that was the problem.

"We're slightly busy here," Sebyl said, frustrated.

"I recommend you listen to her, high priestess," my mother warned from the doorway. The disgust on Sebyl's face made me think I was right about my earlier assumption. Luckily, mom did not care to entertain the childish tantrum the high priestess was having. "It's Cathan," she said. "He's up to something. You need to see this immediately."

The High Coven library looked and smelled exactly as I remembered. Dust settled on the rows of shelves surrounding me, covering glass bottles of potions and ancient looking tomes that beckoned to be read. I pressed my shoulder blades to the cold iron of the spiral staircase and kept a watchful eye on the round table in the center of the room. The usual mess Luna often left after a night of research was gone. There were no books strewn about, no notebook pages spread open, no ingredients for potions in the making. Instead, only one thing lay in the center of the table—an inconspicuous-looking glass jar. Inside the jar, shadows darker than the deepest night swarmed in circles and formed a tiny tornado. With each passing, the jar vibrated and banged against the wooden table so much I was worried it would shatter. As if sensing my discomfort, Luna pressed a forefinger to the top of the jar to steady it and said, "Don't worry, I have the glass spelled. It cannot break." As she removed her finger, the jar tipped over and started rolling down the table until she grabbed hold of it and steadied it again.

"He can roll, though," I said. "Is that his plan? To roll out of here?"

I walked to the table and leaned down until my face was level with the black tornado that was Cathan and tapped on the glass. "You're not going to get out of there, you hear me?"

Luna trained her violet eyes on me. "That is not why we called you."

Without breaking eye contact with me, she stepped away from the table like she was about to present a makeshift volcano for a science fair, and folded her arms across her chest. When I looked at my mom, I realized she had taken on the same stance, her expression just as grim. *Since when were these two twinsies?* Something was about to go down. The jar vibrated again, the shadows inside twirling faster and faster and faster. Sparks ignited around the lid and the crackle almost sounded like fire. Goosebumps crawled across my arms, and I watched in terror as the lid of the jar started to burst into flames.

"We think he's trying his magic in there," my mother explained.

"He doesn't have fire magic."

"No, but we think that he is expanding enough energy trying to break free, and the friction is what is causing the fire. We need to figure something out before he burns this whole place down."

Luna hovered an open palm over the jar and cold wind blew through the basement library, extinguishing the tiny flames. "I can contain the fire with a protective shield for now. Though if he keeps trying, he might blow himself up in there."

Picturing Cathan shattering into a million pieces made me feel all warm and cozy inside, and if I didn't think he'd take down the entire city block with him, I might have let him continue this madness. Goddess, I couldn't even believe I was entertaining the idea. What kind of serial killer mentality was that? To want to see someone in a million pieces?

I shook myself free from the dark shackles of my thoughts. With Cathan gone, so was our chance of saving the paranormals on Earth.

Slowly, I sucked air in through the slit between my teeth. "Let's try it your way."

"You're agreeing to put all our efforts into finding a way to open the portal?" Sebyl asked.

"I am, but you have to agree that before you free the monster, we're going to sit down and find a plan to put him right back in there."

When everyone nodded their agreement, I leaned in closer to the jar and said, "I suppose I better get some rest."

"How can you sleep at a time like this?"

"I can't, but I have to try. I need to get a message to Solen. The fae will need to be convinced to make the journey across, and I have the feeling it will take all of our friends in Faerie to accomplish that. If you think finding the bomb has been tough, you have no idea how hard we're about to work to cross the fae over."

The high priestess didn't look convinced, but I knew that their plan depended on the one thing I had no clue how to do—talking some sense into the fae.

Chapter Eight

Logan

*C*athan's library was a proper mess and made me realize how badly I let the palace fall apart.

Cobwebs collected in every nook and cranny of the vast room. I hadn't realized this realm even had spiders. My thoughts jumbled, and I shivered, thinking about whatever spider-adjacent fae creature might be crawling in the night.

"I'm going to try over there," Savannah called out from behind one bookcase. The palace library had at least fifty rows of books, and was bigger than most libraries I'd seen back on Earth. The books filling the shelves covered any subject you could imagine. From large magical tomes cataloging spells to omnibus collections dealing with paranormal creatures. Some were regular books, same as we had back home, which was refreshing to see. Savannah laughed for almost five minutes when she found a massive book on needle craft. I had to hand it to her, picturing Cathan cross-stitching in his pristine palace was bloody funny.

"Okay, love!" I yelled back. "I'll keep slugging through here."

I didn't know what I was hoping to find. So far, Savannah and I managed to make our way through at least ten rows of shelves, and nothing even remotely mentioning the bomb or portal came up. My eyes lazily scanned the pages of the book on the table depicting hand-drawn images of water fae. Most of them looked an awful lot like Solen, and I wondered if all the males in the water fae line were similar in appearance. The idea seemed so incestuous that I had to force it out of my mind. What was it Korana said about the water fae reproducing? That it doesn't happen as often because it requires too much energy from the realm. I didn't think on it before, but now that Solen had become such a big part of our lives, I couldn't help question everything about him. I didn't trust the bugger. Come to think of it, I didn't trust anyone in Faerie, a trait I picked up from Waverly, who had her guard up at all times.

My head was spinning with visuals of water fae hatching eggs when I noticed a raggedy old spine on one shelf across from me. *Modern Fairytales of Eastern Europe.* I wasn't sure why, but the book called to me. It was as though I had seen it before, despite the fact that this was the first time I'd stepped foot in Cathan's library. I walked toward the book, pulling it from the shelf. It was no more special than any other in the library, and yet as I held it, I felt the wrongness in it. Like it didn't quite belong. *Bollocks. I think this might be an Earth book.*

My grimy fingers formed around the leather binding as I flipped the pages open, expecting to find nothing useful yet again. As soon as I looked inside, I knew this book was different. Writing filled every empty space around the typeset text —notes made with a careful hand. Cathan's, I was certain of it. My heart thundered in my chest and I turned page after page, reading my father's legacy. For the most part, it was a mishmash of thoughts that Cathan jotted down as they came to him. The diary of a madman.

With a bit of time and more eyes on the job, we'd probably be able to piece some of it together. I started to close the book, my eyes catching on a single passage. I froze.

"You might want to come see this!" I yelled out.

Savannah manifested at my side in seconds, and I fought the urge to jump in surprise. For a human, she moved like a bloody ninja, and it often made me wonder if Savannah didn't have some magic in her after all. I looked her up and down, thanking my lucky stars that this gorgeous woman gave me a shot despite me acting like a Muppet when we first met. Today, Savannah wore her hair in a tight braid that loosened at the nape of her neck, allowing her natural curls to fall down the exposed back of her jumpsuit. It took everything in me not to graze a finger across her bare skin.

As my eyes traveled back up her body, I noticed her gaping and cleared my throat. *Right. Get a crack on, lad. And keep it in your pants.*

I handed Savannah the book, and she read out loud the passage I pointed to.

"Crushed garnet, three raw amethysts, seven drops of fae blood..." She trailed off, her eyes widening. "No freaking way! These are the bomb's ingredients!"

"Yes, freaking way," I said. "We got it, love. We actually found something."

Leaning into me, Savannah flipped through the rest of the pages with maddening speed. "But there isn't anything here on how to stop it."

"No, I'm afraid there isn't."

She huffed out a long breath. "So, it's useless then."

"Not necessarily." I took the book back from her and turned to the original page. My eyes focused on the gutter, where more writing consumed the page. The script here was small, so small it was almost illegible, but if I looked close enough, I could make out the words clearly. "Does that look familiar to you?"

Savannah pressed her nose closer to the page and when her lips parted, I knew she saw what I saw. "Beatrix's book? What does he mean by that?"

We stood motionless, yet nothing came to mind. What book could Billie's mother have that Cathan would care for? I was trying to figure it out so hard I felt a sobbing headache form between my temples. Bollocks.

"The Book of Darkness!" Savannah yelled in my ear so loud I thought my eardrums might pop.

I wrinkled my nose and reread the passage again. "It's a stretch, but it could be it."

"Trust me, Logan," she said. "You haven't seen this thing. It has everything in it! There's a reason why the high priestesses hid it from the other witches. The book is dangerous. If Cathan was going to hide anything on Earth in a book, I'd gamble my life this is it."

"I hope you're right," I whispered. "We'll need Solen to pass the message on to Billie."

"I have a message from her myself," a gruff voice said behind us.

I jumped back from Savannah and let out a growl. Leaning against the shelf stood Solen, his eyes even more transparent today, coloring them an eerie shade of gray. The way he crossed his arms made his bulging biceps appear larger, and despite being the current king, I felt intimidated by the fae before me. Which was no surprise, because he could snap me in half if he wanted to. I arched one eyebrow and looked at the markings on his arms, ones I did not understand. I hadn't seen the other water fae with similar marks, and was it me, or was there more of them today?

"Would you like a closer look, my king?" Solen asked.

I would like to slap you silly. "What message did you say you have from Billie?" I asked instead.

"The witch decided to put her efforts into opening the portal. She believes that if she succeeds, she can move the fae across the threshold and spur Cathan into disarming the bomb."

Bugger. I could not believe my ears. Did Solen say what I think he did? This had the High Coven written all over it— either that or River—I wasn't sure which. Billie would never risk letting Cathan go.

Savannah must have had the same thought because she said, "That is seriously insane, even for her."

"If this is her plan, they must be running out of options. My sister would not put people in danger unless there was no other choice." I untucked the book we found in the library from under my arm. "Do you think you can contact her again? We found something that might help them back on Earth."

Solen tipped his chin and smiled. "I'll see if I can get to her as soon as possible. In the meantime, I need you two to come with me."

"Kinda busy here," Savannah said, gesturing to the books.

The water fae did not seem the least perturbed by her attitude, and I wondered if he was used to such behavior from the time he'd been spending with Victoria. The witch was by no means as headstrong as Savannah, but any woman from Earth was a polar opposite to the fae. Either that or he was a better guy than I thought. I swallowed the groan threatening to burst from my lips. I did not want to start liking the bloke.

Lucky for me, Solen made disliking him quite easy.

"Victoria thinks she can open the portal site from this side," he said. "I suggest that you stop wasting time reading stories and follow me."

Chapter Nine

Savannah

*V*ictoria's magic was unlike anything I've ever seen. If this was a fairytale, she'd be the big bad wolf, huffing and puffing as she worked the energy of the surrounding realm. For the first time, as I watched the witch work, I understood what Logan meant about the strangeness of her magic here. The ground moved under my feet, and in the corner of my eye, I noticed vines sprout from the Earth. They shot up and outward, as though Victoria's magic commanded them to life. I laser focused on the clearing we stood in. This was the same place the portal last opened, though it felt different today. There was no glowing blue light, no atmospheric change to signal a doorway; all I saw before me was a witch with her head thrown back and her mouth wide open. Victoria's arms spread out and bursts of magic sparked on her fingertips. A group of glowing sprites buzzed in circles on my right and I shooed them away, concentrating on the epic weirdness in front of me. On the ground, a small circle of random items surrounded the witch, each one reminding me of home. A silver spoon, a worn-out book, a pile of coins, and the rock Logan fished out from inside a tree earlier. All Earth items.

Near to Victoria, keeping a steady watch, stood Solen. His eyes never left the witch, not even to blink. I wracked my brain for information on the water fae, wondering if they blinked in and out of the water. *Get a grip, girl. Who cares if they blink?*

Victoria's brow creased in concentration and I nudged Logan with my elbow, signaling him to pay attention since something was clearly about to go down. The witch reached into one of the many pockets of her flowing dress and pulled something out. I focused my eyes and gulped hard when I saw the reflection of the sun glisten on the edge of a dagger.

"Um, what is she doing?" I asked.

Logan brought a finger to his lips and shushed. "Let's not ruin this, love. She might be onto something this time."

I took in a big breath and held it in my cheeks like a hamster, my eyes laser focusing on the witch. Before us, Victoria lifted the knife and sliced her left palm in a clean cut. The breath I held escaped, and I watched in horror as she repeated the same motion on her right hand. She turned to Solen with wide eyes. Instead of worrying about her bleeding out all over the clearing, the water fae twirled his finger in the air, drawing a symbol, then pointed to the ground. Victoria nodded, and I gagged in my mouth as blood dripped from her open palms down her arms. My arm reached over my shoulder, instinct drawing me to the bow strapped to my back.

"Seriously, what the hell, Logan?"

He didn't have a chance to respond because before I could even finish the question, Victoria slammed her bloody hands to the ground and let out a guttural, inhuman scream.

Her lips tore apart, and I pressed my hands to my ears, my eyes watering from the sound. It grew louder and louder until I swore I heard branches crack around me. This time, instead of the air rippling as it often did when the witch worked her magic, something else occurred. The parts of the Earth her palms touched started to glow. Bright, shimmering purple veins stretching outward—pushing and pulling until they reached the items carefully laid in the circle. My eyes followed one vein that crept toward the silver spoon. When it touched the spoon, the silver thing shot up into the sky like a volcano erupted beneath it. Pure witch energy combined with the energy of Faerie lifted it higher while all around the circle, the other three items burst into the air.

I steeled my gaze and widened my stance. "What the hell is happening?"

"She's transferring energy from the realm," Logan whispered.

"Doesn't she always do that?"

"No," he answered. "Witches use Faerie energy for their spells. Victoria has been tempering with altering that energy, but this is something else. I think she's moving the energy of the realm through her, combining it with her own, then feeding it back to Faerie."

My jaw slacked.

"Like a magical blood transfusion," Logan added, because I really needed that imagery in my head.

Whatever Victoria was playing at, it felt wrong and dirty, but that wasn't the shocking part. What surprised me most was how calm Solen was, almost as though he wanted her to mess with his realm's core existence. Worse, it seemed he may have been the one who taught her the nifty new trick. *Gross.*

My grip tightened around the bow at my side and I used my index finger to snap at the string. Solen shot me a death glare, and I bit the inside of my cheek, snapping the string harder. *If water-boy gives me one more look, he's gonna have a hole in his body where a hole shouldn't be.*

I was about to tell Logan we're having sushi for dinner, when a movement in the corner of my eye caught my attention. My neck swiveled high to the sky—much further than Victoria would have noticed. Directly above her, a tree leaned unnaturally in like the witch's energy was a lasso pulling on it.

"Watch out!"

I dropped my bow to the ground just as a loud snap sounded above us. My feet pushed off the Earth as I took off running toward Victoria. In the sky, a massive tree trunk came barreling down, soaring through the air and rushing for the witch's head. If I couldn't make it in time, she'd be crushed. I willed my muscles to be stronger, my pace to be faster, but I was too far away. My eyes darted up and I saw the tree trunk get larger and larger as it neared its destination.

Burying my heels in, I leapt forward. I threw myself at Victoria, my chest colliding with her shoulder. She yelped as I body-checked her to the side. With my arms cradled around her, I rolled in time to see the tree trunk slam into the ground. Directly in the spot where Victoria sat moments ago.

My breath pummeled my lungs and my heart beat so fast it felt like it would burst right through my ribcage.

"Think you can let go now," Victoria wheezed out. I realized I was still holding her in a deadlock, so I loosened my arms and let them drop to the earth, breathing heavily to catch my breath. The witch climbed off me, seemingly not even a little bothered by the fact that she nearly died.

"You're welcome," I said, and smacked her hand away. "You have a death wish or something?"

"Or something," the witch mumbled.

Her eyes crept slowly to the tree trunk, and I followed her gaze, my tongue feeling suddenly too large for my mouth. In the center of the circle, the trunk lay on an odd angle, the bottom of it torn clean off. I walked closer to it to get a better look. As I approached, I realized the tree looked like someone had sawed it in half. But where was the other part of it? I looked at the witch. "Does that mean the spell worked?"

"I opened a portal, but it closed when you knocked me down."

I scoffed. "You would have died if I didn't."

"Are you telling us that a piece of that tree is now in Shadowhurst?" Logan asked.

"Hopefully," Victoria answered.

No freaking way! The weirdo actually did it. She figured out how to open the portal from here. I couldn't believe what I was hearing, and my hands slapped together in excitement as I jolted my eyes from the tree to the witch. "This is great news, isn't it? If you can open the portal with whatever it is you did," I said, waving my arm around the clearing, "that means we're safe. We can get the fae across and save everyone on Earth."

"Not exactly," Victoria—who was looking a lot more grim than someone who saved every paranormal on Earth—said.

"What is it?" Logan asked. "What's the problem?"

"You are right. I did open the portal. But you're wrong about me being able to save everyone."

My hands shot to my hips and my mouth gaped open. "Excuse you, ma'am?"

"I don't have enough power to open a portal large enough for anyone to get through. What you saw was the extent of what I can do on my own. So unless you want only half of you showing up in Shadowhurst, I'd say this was a massive fail."

Logan eyed her suspiciously, then turned his attention to Solen. "How do we get her more power?"

The water fae rubbed the back of his neck and met Logan's gaze. I didn't fail to notice that he had inched closer to Victoria in the time we'd been talking, the two of them standing so close now their shoulders touched. "You don't need more power, you need more witches," he said.

My heart dropped to my feet. *Boy, did I never think there would come a day when I wished for more witches.*

Chapter
Ten

Billie

"*There's* nothing here."

Peyton shut the Book of Darkness with a thud. Her thickly painted eyes stared me down for answers, and I felt myself shrink from the weight of her expectations. "B, are you sure Solen said to look here?"

"One hundred percent. Both Logan and Savannah are convinced this book has what we need, and you know my brother—he doesn't share unless he's certain."

"Okay, but like maybe he was certain, but wrong."

I looked at the grimoire. Peyton was right to question Solen's information. We had searched this thing inside and out when we tried to save the shadowers from Sebyl and I hadn't seen anything signaling a magical bomb. It was quite possible Logan misinterpreted the clues he found in Cathan's belongings. *Great.* If that was the case, we may as well say our goodbyes, because I was running out of ideas. I reached for the book and dragged it toward me. "Here, let me give it a shot," I said. My fingers grazed the paper and though there was no actual magic in the book, I swore I felt something otherworldly each time I touched it. Perhaps it was because of what the grimoire symbolized to us witches. A history of magic no one could take away, no matter how many of us they burned. Except now I knew how that history I once cherished originated—with our betrayal of the fae—and my insides turned with disgust each time I remembered the true story behind our magic.

I cracked the book open, laying it flat on Peyton's bed, and crossed my legs. As I flipped through the dusty grimoire, I didn't notice anything out of the ordinary. A few protection spells, some summonings of greater energy, illusion rituals. Just your regular run-of-the-mill magic— nothing that stood out or screamed danger like a magical bomb spell would. My finger touched the edge of the book and I yelped, pulling away. I looked at the giant paper cut right in the center of my thumb and sucked in a sharp breath. Blood pooled on the cut and my eyes darted to a red spot on the book where it had stained the pages.

"Oh, no! Sebyl is going to kill me when she finds this."

"No stress," Payton said with a smile. "Let me grab a tissue and we'll clean it up."

She started to leave and paused. Before us, light shimmered across the book's pages, starting at the spot where my blood soaked into the paper and spreading outward. My jaw hit the ground while Payton stood beside me, motionless. We watched the golden glitter cover the entire book and pile in the center where a page grew like a leaf.

"What in the actual hell?" Payton whispered between clenched teeth. When the bright light dispersed, leaving a new page behind, she grabbed the book off the bed and shoved it in her face. "It's totally blank, girl."

My brow creased. "You don't think my blood had something to do with it?"

"Um, did you see how this thing reacted when you bled all over it?"

I shoved her with my elbow. "I didn't bleed all over it. I got a paper cut."

"You should, you know, get one again," Peyton teased.

My gaze jumped to hers and a lump formed in my throat. I tied my hair back into a messy bun and reached for the hidden compartment in my boot, pulling out the dagger stashed there. Briskly, I pressed the cool metal to the inside of my palm and pulled, wincing. A burning sensation spread from my palm all the way up my arm as my body registered the cut. Eyes wide open, I slammed my palm on the blank page and waited. I didn't have to wait long. Golden light appeared instantaneously, covering the page with its magical paintbrush. Everywhere the light touched, words formed. The script was small and as I inched closer to the page, I realized I recognized the handwriting. "Cathan," I said under my breath. "Looks like Logan and Savannah were onto something, after all."

Peyton and I waited impatiently for the magic to finish working. We put the book between us and read:

"When far from home and left no choice,
There is one reason to rejoice,
Hid in a world that is unkind,
Four sacred elements; this one to bind.
Where traitorous souls rest weary heads,
And secrets lie under their beds,
You start your journey on the stoop
Of the tight-knit and poisonous group.

Beware the night and carry on
Until you reach the trail beyond.
Ignore the links that bind the space,
For oak-lined paths carry your grace.
On that one night of every year
When children gather without fear,
Where cotton mouths are always full,
Their lips turn blue from weather cool.
Follow the steps of those before,
Their scurried feet running to shore.
Beyond the stone and glass, you'll see,
The darkest dark beholds the key."

I turned the page over, looking for more, but that was all we got.

"Oh, good," Peyton said. "Your dad left you a nursery rhyme."

"Don't call him my dad, please." I groaned. "What do you think any of it means?"

Peyton didn't answer. Instead, she ran out of the room and I heard rustling down the hallway. There was a loud bang followed by cursing before she returned with what looked to be a dozen paperbacks in her hand.

"What are those?"

"OMG! Don't even get me started!" Peyton screeched, tossing the stack of books on the bed. "My mom has been on this crazy kick, reading a mystery series." She opened two books and pointed down. "See? I think the whole point of the series is that every book has a riddle the detective has to follow. Like clues on a map or something. It's a game of cat-and-mouse, and my mom eats it up. But it gets her off my back about Morgan, so I'm totally fine with it."

I laughed. "You're saying Cathan left a riddle with clues for us to find?"

"Oh, not for us. But if he left a fail-safe hidden in the Book of Darkness—the last place anyone would check—he wouldn't spell it out. In case someone did come looking."

It did sound like Cathan to go out of his way to make this particular page hard to find. If I hadn't accidentally cut my finger, it never would have occurred to me to use my blood to discover it. I felt instantly foolish. My blood was his blood; I should have at least given it some thought. Pushing the mental flailing aside, I turned my attention back to the rhyme on the page. "Let's see if we can figure this out," I said. "How hard can it be to solve a riddle?"

It turned out that solving riddles was much harder than I imagined. After a couple hours of getting nowhere and feeling absolutely stupid, Peyton and I brought in reinforcements. Soon after we called, Morgan and River poured into the room and crowded Peyton's bed, each one with a notepad in hand and a serious look on their face.

"Okay, this part here, *the stoop of the poisonous group.*" River said. "That has to be the townhouse, right? The traitors are the witches. At least as far as Cathan is concerned."

I looked over the sentence again. "That would make sense. The townhouse is the starting point. Let's put that down."

"Already on it!" Morgan and Peyton chimed in unison. They flattened out a map of Stamwick on the bedroom floor and drew a big red X where the townhouse should be.

"Good. That's good," I said. "So, if this references the

townhouse, then *oak-lined paths* might refer to the park down the street."

Morgan drew another X on the map.

"On the one night of every year when children gather without fear. I don't get this part. What could that mean?"

River scratched his chin while Peyton and Morgan exchanged blank faces. *I should know this.* I grew up in Stamwick; the park was one I frequented not only as a child, but as a grown witch. I shivered thinking of all the shadowers I vanquished there. Tearing myself from painful memories, I concentrated on the rhyme in the book. "Wait!" I announced, looking over the following two lines again. *Where cotton mouths are always full, their lips turn blue from weather cool.* Something bothered me about the way they were phrased. They sounded too odd and clunky for Cathan's royal tongue. I reached for my phone, pulling up a map of the park. My fingers zoomed in and out as I navigated the city's streets. There was something so familiar about the area, and I couldn't quite put my finger on it. "No way..." I said, as realization dawned on me. "The Santa Claus parade!"

My friends looked at me like I had lost my mind and I brushed them off, turning my attention back to the phone. "Every year there's a massive, over-the-top Santa Claus parade in Stamwick," I explained. "It's a big deal in the city. Everybody shows up! I remember going as a kid. I think Beatrix took me."

"I guess Cathan was a fan of the holidays."

I smacked River. "It's not the parade that's important. To prepare for it, they decorate the performers' walk areas. There are lights and ribbons and garlands lining the streets. It's beautiful! But my favorite part was always the cotton candy machines. We stood in line for hours to get some, and I distinctly remember shivering from the cold."

"No freaking way!" Peyton yelled. "That has to be it! Do you think you could map out the route?"

"I can do one better," I said, scrolling through the internet. "The parade route hasn't changed in fifty years and there's a map of it on the city's website."

Referencing the map on my phone, I used a black marker to draw a line where the parade started and ended—right in the center of the Financial District. "This is it," I said. "But it doesn't explain the last line. *The darkest dark beholds the key.*"

My pulse raced in my veins and I could feel my temples throb. We were so close, I could taste it. Around me, my friends fidgeted in their seats as they tried to solve the last part of the riddle. For a moment, I felt like the detective in Peyton's books; clever enough to outsmart the killer. My body stood stone still. This wasn't a story, and I wasn't playing make-believe. Lives depended on us following Cathan's trail, and I hated every second of it. I had grown sick and tired of playing his games, and yet here I was, smack-dab in the middle of another one. The bastard was toying with me even while he was imprisoned.

River took the marker from my hand and drew a big circle where the Stamwick Pier was. "Got it."

"Why would the riddle lead us to the pier?" I asked at same time as Morgan said, "Crap!"

She snatched the Book of Darkness and re-read the riddle again and again until the words tangled together as she spoke. "It says '*four elements; this one to bind.*' What does that sound like to you?"

"A circle casting," I said.

"Exactly! *This one to bind!* If we think of this page as the uniting element, the first one, then we have four more to find to cast the circle."

My eyes narrowed. "You think Cathan hid another page of the book at the pier? For the water element."

Morgan nodded. I looked at my friend's eager face and smiled. We were on the right track; I could feel it. *You're not as clever as you think you are,* I thought. For the first time I was relieved to be that monster's daughter, because if there was any part of him in me, I would find it and use it to take him down.

Chapter Eleven

Billie

*B*y the time we reached the pier, the sun had begun to set as the moon rose on the horizon. Nobody bothered to make stops—not even for backup. As soon as we solved the riddle, we hopped into River's car and made our way to Stamwick. We were in such a hurry, I had completely forgotten to tell the Chandlers I wouldn't be back for dinner. Sending a quick text to Imala, I pocketed my phone and grabbed River's hand. "Where do you guys want to start?"

The pier seemed larger than life when one didn't know what to look for. I wondered if we made the mistake of not planning things out a bit better; coming back in the morning when we were refreshed and had more time to scour the nooks and crannies of the vast space.

"Why don't we start at that end," Peyton yelled over her shoulder, "and you two get the other side?"

Agreeing, we proceeded to part ways. As I watched Peyton and Morgan's backs retreat, nausea filled my gut. Something didn't feel right. Why would Cathan hide a page from the book where any human can find it? It didn't make any sense. I must have stopped walking because River pulled on my sleeve to get my attention.

I shook myself into alertness. "Sorry, I'm thinking."

"Care to share?"

"It doesn't track for him to hide the page here. Not when anyone could stumble upon it."

I kicked over an empty takeout container and scanned the pier. The night brought in a heavy fog and I wondered if we were due for rain. The last thing I wanted was to be trapped here in the dark and soaking wet. My teeth chattered as the chill of the evening permeated my bones as I huddled close to River, welcoming the perma-heat of his body.

"Could he have spelled it?" River asked.

"Cathan doesn't do spells. He's fae. Plus, the entire time he was on Earth he was in shadow form, so how did he even get the page here in the first place?"

Bile rolled into my throat as I considered one possible answer to that question. No, it couldn't be. Beatrix would not help him do this, no matter how in love with him she was. One thing my mom and I had in common was we asked a lot of questions. If Cathan asked her to hide something, she would have wanted to know what it was and why it needed to be hidden. I looked around, unsettled.

"You don't think we'll find anything, do you?"

"No," I admitted. "What if we got it wrong? What if the riddle didn't point to the pier? Worse, what if it didn't point anywhere at all and we're reaching for straws?"

I paused, my toes wiggled in my boots as I pressed my feet into the decking. With no witch to help Cathan, he must have used fae magic. He may not have had a lot of power on Earth, but he had his shadows and the energy they provided. I gagged, thinking back to my time in the cave and how he tricked me. If he could do that, who knew what else his shadows could do? I closed my eyes and reached for my own shadows, coaxing them out from hiding and letting them burst free of the confines of my body. They crawled the pier and covered every bench, every plank of the walkway, making the night seem even darker. Even the streetlamps evaporated in their midst.

From further down the pier, Peyton yelled out, "What's going on?"

"Don't worry," I called back. "It's only me trying something out."

"Awesome sauce!"

Snapping my eyes wide open, I pulled the rest of the shadows from within me and forced them out. River clung to my back, using me as a guide in the darkness.

"See anything yet?"

I sighed. "Not yet." My head swiveled, surveying the pier, when a speck of light caught my attention on the horizon. "Wait, I think I got something."

My legs pumped until I was almost running toward the light. In my veins blood rushed at a thunderous pace. I gulped air as I rushed forward, convinced we found something useful. An arm wrapped around my waist and yanked me backward. My breath froze in my lungs and I lost hold of my magic, the shadows settling back deep down at the base of my belly.

My back pressed against a hard surface and it took me a second to realize it was River's chest. I looked back, then followed the direction River glared. He caught me moments before I walked myself off the pier and straight into the water.

"Close call," River said, and brushed his lips against the base of my neck. "Where were you going so fast?"

I pointed to the water. "There was a light there."

"It's probably a boat."

"The shadows would not illuminate anything human. This was magic. It was faint, but it was there. I think Cathan hid the next clue in the river."

River uncoiled his arms from around my waist and ran his fingers through his hair. His green eyes darkened, and I felt his chest puff out as he breathed in the night air. Behind us, feet shuffled as Peyton and Morgan closed the distance between them and the water. I smiled. "Anyone up for a midnight swim?"

"Are you sure this is okay?" Morgan asked for the hundredth time.

I smiled reassuringly. "They won't even know it's missing. Promise."

The fake positivity was for Morgan's sake and Morgan's sake only. While I had every intention of returning the boat I had magically jump-started in one piece, we all knew that when it came to me, things didn't always go according to plan. Waves splashed around us and we battled the water, aiming for the spot I saw the light. Our eyes scanned every inch of the murky dark, and so far, the only lights we saw were buoys and the reflection of the city lights behind us. It was beginning to look like whatever it was I thought I saw was a figment of my imagination. Disappointment laced through me as I lowered my head, dropping my gaze to my feet. "Should I try the shadows again?" I asked.

"NO!" everyone yelled out in unison.

River wiped water from his jeans. "It's hard enough to navigate as it is. If you make it any darker, we won't see where we're going. I don't want to crash into another boat in case there is one out here." I nodded in agreement. "We'll go as far as that buoy over there and then turn around, okay?"

My hopes deflated, and I didn't bother saying anything else. Heart aching, I let my hand drop off the edge of the boat, my fingers scraping the surface of the water. The coolness of it sent shivers down my spine, and I swallowed hard, my legs tensing. My eyes watered as a sudden sting burned my palm, right where I sliced it open with the dagger. My hand felt like it was on fire. The water was no longer cold and comforting but scorching, as though I had dipped my hand in a vat of acid. I grit my teeth together, fighting against the pain.

"What's wrong?" River asked through our bond.

"All good. There's something here, I think. Slow down," I answered. I opened my mouth to explain what I felt moments ago, but my words cut off.

"Watch out!" Morgan yelled out in warning.

I thrust my hand out of the water, but I was too slow. Blue, scaly fingers wrapped over my arm and pulled me in. My balance failed, and I tripped over the edge of the boat, hitting the surface of the water headfirst. Above, commotion rose from our boat, and I watched River's face peer over the edge. He got smaller and smaller as whatever held my wrist dragged me into the depths of the river. We dropped further down until all I saw was blackness. I yanked my arm, pulling against whatever held me, but there was no use. Whatever this thing was, it was stronger than me. Slowly, my will to breathe subsided, and I let my arms float to the sides as I sank to the bottom. *This is fine. I want this.* My arm burned, reminding me of where I was. I shook my head, the messy bun atop it coming undone. My hair floated around me, obscuring my vision. I knew this feeling of giving up—I remembered it like it was yesterday. It was the same feeling I had when I was nearly drowned by the water fae in Faerie.

It can't be! My eyes snapped wide open, and I jerked my head to look at the creature holding me. Taloned nails tore at my flesh, and I followed the fae's slim, scale-covered arm all the way to its sunken face and eyes threaded with green. The fae hissed, water bubbling around her toothy mouth, and pushed her body closer to mine. I brought my knee to my chest and kicked, slamming my boot into her rancid face. My free arm reached into the back of my boot, pulling out a dagger. Fingers wrapping over the hilt, I sliced the dagger through the murky water, aiming for the fae. The nasty creature shoved her face in mine—two rows of sharp teeth snapping, giving me the chance I needed. I swung the dagger, but the fae swirled out of the way, her long legs looping around my body and knocking me sideways. The dagger broke free of my grip and my throat closed up as I watched it sink to the bottom of the river. The fae swam in circles around me. Each path she made, she got closer and closer, hissing like a wildcat. My vision flickered as the lack of oxygen attacked my body and when the fae jumped toward me, her nails pointed, I pulled my body backward.

That was a mistake.

The last of the air in my lungs escaped, and I fought the urge to breathe in river water. My eyes failed me. I blinked to keep them in focus, spotting the strange locket around the fae's neck. The symbol was familiar; it was the same one I used when working water magic. I wanted to reach for her, to pull the locket from her neck, but my strength depleted. I was drowning. My lids grew heavy, like they were made of lead, and as they closed, I made my peace that this was how I ended.

Through half-shut lids, I saw a figure, then another. Someone held the fae back while the other placed a hand atop her head. The water fae squirmed and screeched as she fought against the person holding her. The view before me swam in and out of focus. Peyton. I saw Peyton press her fingers into the fae's forehead and push her magic out. Slowly the thrashes came to a stop and the creature's glowing eyes closed.

River wrapped his arm around me, and I realized he was holding me with one hand this entire time. With the small amount of strength I had left, I pointed to the necklace hanging off my neck, then down toward the fae. *"Get that locket,"* I thought into our bond. River repeated my motion to Peyton, and my best friend dove without question. My body grew rigid, and pain, unlike any other, spread through every inch of it. I couldn't wait much longer. My lips parted instinctually, and I sucked in a ragged breath, dirty water pouring into my lungs.

I heard water splash and the cold air of the night hit my face. Hands grabbed my arms and dragged me upward, and I landed with a thud on the boat's hard bottom. Rough palms pumped into my chest, then River's lips pressed to mine.

Air. Sweet, sweet air crowded my system, and I shot up to sit, water flowing from my mouth as I coughed. My entire body felt like someone punched me repeatedly. I rested my arms over my knees and took a deep breath as Peyton reached over the boat's edge and pulled herself up.

"Girl, I did not sign up for this!" She wrung out the bottom of her shirt and growled. "This was my favorite outfit."

"The locket! Did you get the locket?" I asked.

Peyton's wicked smile spread and she threw her hand up, opening her fingers one by one. In her palm, a silver locket shined in the light of the moon. I sighed in the relief, reaching for it, but Peyton shut her fist around the necklace before I could touch it. She pointed a finger at me. "Yeah, finders keepers."

My best friend reached around and pulled out something else from the back of her jeans. I laughed when I spotted the dagger I dropped. When did Peyton become a treasure diver? A click rang out through the boat as she slid the dagger's blade into the locket and undid the clasp. Slowly, she reached in to pull something out. All three of us leaned closer to watch Peyton unfold a cream piece of paper.

"It's blank."

I reached around and snatched the paper from her hands, turning it over. The edges were torn, but not by a careless hand. I shimmied to the bag I left in the boat before the damn fae pulled me under and pulled out the Book of Darkness. The right edge of the paper we found in it wasn't as smooth as the other sides, and as I brought the new piece of paper toward it, I realized the torn sides matched. I glanced up at Peyton, then wedged the two pieces together. Sparkling magic brightened the night. It traveled over the book, revealing text on the new page I added. I read the words, my heart sinking to my toes. *Wonderful, another damn riddle.*

Chapter Twelve

Billie

"Watch for the one whose death is near,
In open eyes, without a fear,
Whose shiny baubles on display
Harbor more trouble than they claim.
Then count to five toward the sound
Of breaking waves and boisterous crowds,
Between the rocks that hold you blind,
The turquoise gem hides what you'll find."

"Well, that's ominous," Morgan said, cringing.

Peyton reached over and tucked a loose strand of hair behind her ear. "Was it the death part that threw you off?"

"And pretty much everything else."

I shivered, my body recovering from the cold water that soaked my clothes and chilled me down to the bone. I glanced at the riddle again, then turned my head to look out into the darkness of the river. My pulse thundered in my veins and my head felt like somebody had tightened a vise around it. I crossed my arms and trained my eyes on the river. "How is there a water fae on Earth?" I asked.

River shrugged. "And how long has it been here?"

That was a really great question. Considering the riddle we found in the locket, I would think the water fae had been on Earth long before I was even born, probably around the time Cathan hid all these clues on Earth, maybe even as far back as centuries ago. But how did the High Coven not know of the fae's existence? And how did it get here from Faerie?

If the story Beatrix told us was true and she was the one to open the portal, it stood to reason the fae came through during her time in Stamwick. Though that couldn't be right. My mother would have noticed if someone sneaked across while she was visiting Cathan. She told me herself she took the utmost care to make certain she wasn't detected by the High Coven; there must have been another way the fae got into our realm. My blood boiled. Did Cathan bring that poor creature to this realm, and separated her from her kind to hide his little riddles? The air must have dropped a few degrees because I was suddenly even colder than before. I wouldn't have been surprised to find out that was exactly what the King of Faerie did.

"Do you think that tracks, babe?" River asked, jarring me from my thoughts.

I looked at him, bewildered. "Sorry, can you repeat that?"

"The part about the shiny baubles; we're thinking it might mean a museum or gallery."

"I'm not sure," I said. "Could be, but I don't know. This riddle is more convoluted than the first one. And what is the gem he's referring to? An actual gem? Like a crystal?"

I looked from River to the others, who had about as much

a clue as I did. It was starting to look like the riddles would get harder with each turn, if there were more of them out there, as we guessed. If we couldn't figure out the second one, what chance did we have of solving them all? My stomach turned, and I ran a finger over the parchment in my hands, praying to the Goddess for some clue and receiving nothing in return.

"I hate to break up this party, but I think we all need to rest," Peyton said. Her shirt was wet and her hair clung to her face in black and red streaks. With her mascara running down her face, she looked like she about had it with tonight.

They probably all did.

"She's right," River agreed. "We should get a move on. "Why don't we get photos of the riddle and sleep on it? We can reconvene in the morning."

I didn't want to sleep on it. I wanted to solve the damn riddle right there and then. We were beyond running out of time, and I knew sleep would not come easy tonight. If at all. One look at my friends told me I was an idiot. Each one of them appeared more exhausted than I felt. If they didn't get rested up, they'd be useless tomorrow when it was time to follow the trail. I pressed my lips into a thin line and said, "Let's go home."

River dropped me off at the Chandlers' right as the sun was rising and I tiptoed through the quiet house, my boots under my arm and my feet barely touching the hardwood floors, then ran across the backyard to the guest house. Mind racing, I fell into the silk covers of the bed and, for the first time in what seemed like ages, let the ache in my body melt away.

My fingers reached into my jeans' pocket and I pulled out the piece of paper Cathan left behind, reading it again. There was no way I could sleep right now, so I may as well make myself useful.

"*Watch for the one whose death is near. In open eyes, without a fear.* What the hell are you talking about, Cathan?" Saliva pooled in my mouth and I swallowed it down, reading the next two lines. "*Whose shiny baubles on display harbor more trouble than they claim.*"

No way was Cathan talking about a museum. A lot of places hold baubles on display, but something about the first riddle bugged me. It felt personal, like the places he picked meant something to him. Or to Beatrix. My toes curled, and I froze, staring at the handwriting. The fog on my brain lifted and my eyes widened as the answer formed in my mind. I shot up and turned to my nightstand, tearing the small drawer open and rummaging through until my fingers clutched the necklace Ms. Broussard gave me when I first arrived in Shadowhurst. I squeezed the clasp between my two fingers and brought it closer to my face, inspecting the tiny inscription carved into the metal.

"Handmade with love," I read aloud.

My heart raced and my skin felt tighter; like I was wearing a sweater two sizes too small. I reached for my phone, dialing River's number. He answered on the first ring.

"I was about to call you," River said. "Couldn't sleep either, huh?"

"Not a wink," I admitted. "But I know what the first few lines of the riddle mean. I think he's talking about the Crystal Cauldron. When he's talking about death being near, he must mean her old age. And she is a huge witch supporter and doesn't hide it."

River hissed out a breath on the other end. "What about the baubles? Why are they trouble?"

"Because they're not tourist traps like the shop leads you to believe. Everything inside the Crystal Cauldron is a conduit for witches. When I first got here, it was my main go-to for the supplies I needed to cast spells."

For a few minutes, there was complete silence on the line. I thought we may have been disconnected until I heard River say, "Count to five. Five miles?"

"What's five miles from the Crystal Cauldron that's notable?"

River was silent again, and I knew he was pulling up a map of Shadowhurst on his phone. He tapped something and hummed a tune I didn't know as he searched. Then suddenly, he gasped, and I almost dropped my phone from the shock. "What is it?"

"Waves, crowds, rocks that keep you blind from the rest of the town... what does it all sound like to you?"

"Oh my Goddess..."

"The quarry," River whispered. "The turquoise gem is the Shadowhurst Quarry. You up for a drive?"

I was already standing. "I'm not far from there," I said. "It will be faster if I bike over."

"Meet you at the quarry in fifteen. And be careful."

I was about to hang up when a thought occurred to me. "Why don't you give Raiden and Mel a call and tell them to be on standby? Just in case."

With that, I pushed the door of the guesthouse open and rushed to the next destination.

On this particular morning, unlike the last few times I'd been there, the quarry was eerie as hell. My mind recalled the first time I came by with Peyton. Memories of academy students crowding the beach, their laughter carrying across the water as they splashed around. Today, however, there was not one person in the quarry. Even the birds that often perched on the trees were gone. I looked at my watch, realizing how early it was.

"Where do you want to start?" River asked. I pointed to the waterfall. "Seems like the best place."

I was about to take my shoes off and wade into the water when River grabbed my hand and pulled me to the right. "There's a small pass this way. Savannah and I used to hide away here when we were younger."

We walked down the beach, and my feet sank into the sand almost all the way to my ankles with every step. Behind us, the sun rose higher in the sky, making the quarry water sparkle like raw turquoise. My mind immediately went to the riddle, and I cringed, hating that Cathan described this place exactly as I would have. I trudged behind River, sticking closer to the quarry walls as the beach we walked on narrowed. Right when I thought we would run out of space, I noticed a few flat stones appear at the edge of the sand. If you stepped carefully, they formed a makeshift walkway trailing all the way behind the waterfall. I placed my foot on the first one, then the next, mimicking River's motions. The water fell from above at a rising speed, splashes of it going in my eyes and blurring my vision. I wiped my eyes with the rear of my hand and looked ahead. A gasp escaped me.

To my left, the waterfall stood as a wall, hiding us from the quarry, while to our right a vast space opened as the rock formation gave way to a small indent in the quarry walls. A few discarded beer cans lay on the ground, and I spotted an empty bag of chips in the corner. With how secluded the hiding spot was, it made sense for this to be party central for high school kids. I gagged in my mouth and tried not to think of the endless make-out sessions that must have taken place here late at night.

"Don't be weird," River said. "It's a place to hang out, that's all."

I opened my mouth to argue, but before I could utter a word, the wall started to shake. Dust fell on our heads and I stutter-stepped, falling backward toward the rushing water. River's hand reached for my leather jacket, and he dragged me toward him, pressing me into his hard chest. As we cowered together in the center of the crevice and worked to avoid the massive boulders pelleting around us, a sense of danger emanated from my stomach. A rock the size of my arm in diameter plummeted down and we swerved in unison out of its way. My shadows shot outward, wrapping around River and me in protection. They swirled over us, shielding us from the falling debris, but my magic was of no use. Since when did Shadowhurst have earthquakes? Something wasn't sitting well with me as I considered another reason we might be in this situation. Something was shaking the Earth hard enough to cause all this chaos. Maybe it wasn't the rocks we should worry about. I shuddered, a scream hanging off my lips as I watched a horned Earth fae step around the water-fall and charge for us.

Chapter Thirteen

River

The green bastard lunged for Billie and I pulled her away in time, twisting us closer to the quarry wall. The fae's size was unlike any I'd seen before, probably one of the largest and towering close to ten feet tall, and I wondered how the hell something so big could stay hidden on Earth. And at the quarry, of all places! The fae slipped, missing us by mere inches. He rebounded quickly for someone his size, spinning on his heels to face us. Steam billowed from his nostrils, and he kicked the dirt back with his massive feet. Between the horns and the predatory behavior, the fae looked more like a bull than a person.

Hiding Billie behind me, I looked at the fae, noticing the scars on his arms and legs. His skin didn't look like skin at all. Moss covered almost every inch of it and for a second, I felt bad for the guy. It looked painful.

That second came and passed pretty quickly because before I knew it, the damn fae jumped for us again. I tried to pull Billie out of the way, but she had other plans.

The shadows that were keeping us safe burst, only to

reform again in front of the fae barreling toward us. He wavered for a moment, staring fearfully at Billie's magic.

At least the damn thing is afraid of something.

Billie pointed a finger, and the shadows swirled around the fae in a wild tornado of magic, encompassing him in a nightly prison. The Earth fae lowered his horns, piercing through Billie's magic. A muscled leg came crashing down, and the ground shook beneath us. My eyes lowered to see the ground split. It shook harder and harder and I had to press my palm to the rocky wall to keep from falling. My nails gripped at the wet slime and I gagged, one hand reaching for Billie's jacket. I tugged on it. "Babe, I don't think it's working. We should make a run for it."

"Not yet," she said.

What the hell does she have in mind now? Billie always had a plan and her plans always worked, but not before getting us into deep trouble.

I watched in horror as she dropped to the ground, her hand pressing into the earth beneath. Her eyes rolled to the back of her head and the ground stopped shaking instantly. Earth magic. *She's using the fae's tricks against him!* The cracks spreading on the ground and heading toward us halted, changing directions. My gaze knifed to the fae, who watched the cracks race for him in confusion. *He doesn't know how she can wield his power,* I thought. Inside me, the wolf came alive, and I dropped down, ready to shift.

"*Don't,*" Billie warned through our bond.

Before I could ask her why, she leapt for the fae. I wasn't sure who was more confused, me or the green giant. His eyes narrowed to slits as my girl ran toward him at full speed. Her wrists flicked inward, and she commanded her shadows to leave the fae and crawl back into her body. As Billie got closer, the fae readied to attack, and my heart jumped into my throat.

"Babe!" I yelled out.

Billie didn't stop.

She dropped to the ground mid run and slid across the wet rocks, right in between the fae's legs. As she slipped through, she latched onto something on the fae's ankle. "Are those shackles?"

I received no answer, of course. Billie's free hand went up, and I caught a glimpse of a sharp, jagged rock in it. Before the fae could react, she crashed her hand into the shackle on his left leg. Shadows burst on the impact, covering the shackle entirely. The fae paused. I did too. For a moment nothing happened, but then a loud bang sounded as the shackle tore apart and fell to the ground. Billie looked up at the fae, and when he made no movement to stop her, she freed his other leg.

My jaw gaped. "What's going on?"

Billie got up, dusting herself off and stood in front of the fae. "Is that better?" she asked.

The fae nodded. "Thank you."

"Seriously, what the hell?" I asked.

Billie looked at me over her shoulder, her hair wild and knotted, a mixture of water and earth muddying up her face. From here she looked like she was ready for war, but she stood calmly next to the fae that tried to kill us. "He was chained," she said and pointed to the broken shackles.

"I have been here for centuries. No one has been able to do what you did," the fae said mournfully.

"Has anyone tried?"

"No, I'm afraid not."

The sadness in his face unnerved me and I found it difficult to reconcile having this conversation with wanting to kill the horned man only moments ago. "Why are you shackled down?" I asked. "And why couldn't you break free? You look strong enough to do it."

"I did not have the magic required to open the locks," the fae explained. "Only one of our kind could."

"Cathan," Billie said. "His shadow magic was the answer."

"Yes, yes, it was. The king deemed that I should stay behind, and so I had to stay, no matter my own choice."

"What do you mean, behind?" I asked.

The fae leaned against the quarry wall and slid down until his long legs dangled on the ground before him. In this position, he looked much weaker than I first thought—more broken. It was official: Cathan was a bigger asshole than I gave him credit for. To imprison one of his own was another level of bastard. At least the water fae we encountered didn't seem to have suffered as this man did. My chest hurt. We killed her. She could have been a victim of Cathan's bullshit, and we killed her.

The fae rubbed his temples and sighed. "When the portal closed, those of us on this side were to return home, but the king requested we stay behind. I did not wish to stay. He disagreed."

Billie covered her mouth with her hand and gasped. "You're one of the original fae that held the magic between Earth and Faerie, aren't you?"

"I am."

My voice quivered, but I asked, "Was there a water fae here with you? A gnarly looking woman, vicious as hell?"

"Ah! You mean Illyria. She was one as well, though she actually wanted to remain. I'd steer clear of her if you have the chance. Illyria is not one to make friends. At least not one she hasn't tried to kill yet."

That did not make me feel any better about her fate.

"Unlike me," the fae continued, "Illyria did not have anyone to go back to. She was more than willing to infect your realm with her presence."

My stomach turned. "You have a family?"

"I did."

"And that bastard trapped you here and away from them? Did he say why?" I asked, even though I already knew the answer.

The fae's expression dropped, and he reached over to pick up one of the shackles. "He said he'll need something protected in the future and to be ready when he returned for me." His massive fingers pulled the metal apart, and he reached in, pulling out a piece of parchment. He handed it to Billie and said, "You have the same magic as him."

"Unfortunately, yes," Billie answered. "Your king, Cathan, is my father."

The fae grimaced.

"Don't worry, I'm nothing like him. In fact, you don't have to fear him anymore. He's currently... incapacitated."

Relief flooded the fae's features. "You mean I can return to my family? To my children?"

I must have made a noise because Billie shot me a deadpan stare that told me to keep myself together. I couldn't help it. My blood boiled thinking about how much I wanted to tear Cathan's limbs off. Maybe when this was all over, I'd finally get to. Teeth bared, I snapped my jaw shut and willed myself to relax. "Not exactly," I said. "But we're hoping that what you've been guarding could help us get you home. Or get your family here."

Carefully, Billie unfolded the piece of parchment. She reached into her bag and removed the Book of Darkness, laying it flat on the ground. Kneeling, she placed the new parchment next to the double spread we'd completed, and a brilliant light illuminated the space we stood in. As the parchment fused itself to the rest of the page, the fae's golden eyes widened and he stared down, amazed at the magic before him. I couldn't blame him. The process was pretty freaking cool.

Right on cue, words appeared on the page, a new riddle. More clues.

Billie swallowed hard and read:

> "In a hurry to escape,
> Seek the one that holds no shape.
> Fairy lights to guide your way
> And keep your steps hidden away.
> Wind at your back, the darkness calls,
> Cross your fingers where it falls."

As she spoke the words, I typed them on my phone into a group chat, ending with instructions for the girls to get more eyes on the riddle. Now that we were back at Shadowhurst, it wouldn't hurt to involve the group. The faster we could solve this thing, the better, and since I didn't have any ideas on where Cathan led us this time, I wanted to bring in the cavalry. I told Peyton and Morgan to head to the resistance house and that we would meet them there shortly. As I pressed *send*, I felt Billie's breath on my neck and turned to see her looking at the message approvingly.

I chuckled. *My little control freak.*

"This is going to help get me home?" the Earth fae asked.

Billie smiled. "Hopefully. In the meantime, why don't we get you somewhere safe? I'm sure you'll be glad to be free of this place. I'm Billie, by the way." She reached out her small hand, and the fae took it, obscuring her fingers from view with his mammoth palm.

"Malakai," he said. "It's a pleasure to meet you."

He looked at me and I tipped my chin. "I'm River. I have some people I'd like for you to meet."

Chapter
Fourteen

Billie

"*I*t's the hiking trails," Mel said nonchalantly, not looking at anyone in particular.

We sat on the front porch of the house, scratching our heads trying to solve the latest riddle. Seeing Raiden's proud smile told me Mel got it. I couldn't believe she figured it out so quickly; we'd been at this for less than an hour.

I peeled my bottom lip off the floor. "How can you be so sure?"

"Oh, it's easy," the lion shifter responded. "The one that holds no shape is wind. Wind doesn't hold any shape. He's talking about the old windmill by the bus station. For sure."

"And the escape part?"

"The bus, obviously," she answered. "It's the only bus out of Shadowhurst if you don't count the train station. But there are no windmills there."

I bit the inside of my cheek and looked at the page on the table. We were getting closer to completing it, and yet I wasn't as excited as I should be. The hours were ticking away and we wouldn't have enough time left if this was a dead end. What if the riddles were another game Cathan played to waste our time so we couldn't discover the real bomb? I shook my head. No, that couldn't be it. I refused to believe it. This was much too planned out to be a coincidence. Cathan didn't do coincidences.

Reading the riddle again, I focused my attention on Mel. "Do you think the Faerie lights could be—"

"The lamps on the hiking trail," she cut me off. "Definitely. They're near the windmill and those trails can hide a person pretty well."

I smiled, satisfied that we were finally onto something. "How are you so good at this?"

"Riddles were a big deal at my house when I was growing up."

A darkness passed over her features, and I wondered if there was more to the story but didn't press it. Mel was not the kind of woman you forced answers from. Even when she wasn't in her lion form, she'd rip your head off for asking, which was one of the traits I admired most about her. Fierce with a capital F.

I left the question lingering in my mind and looked down at the paper in my lap. "What do you think the cross means?"

"Jeez, kid! Are you serious?" She looked at me like I was a complete fool and I bit my tongue until I tasted iron, careful not to say anything that would upset her. On any other day, I'd have talked back, but today, Mel was our best chance of solving this damn thing and since neither River nor I had any ideas, I wasn't about to ruin a good thing. Unclenching the fists at my side, I flat-palmed the table. "Dead serious," I answered sweetly.

"It's the church cross," the shifter said. "Cross your fingers. Get it?"

My face paled at how stupid I felt.

"The darkness falling could be the shadow the cross casts," Mel said, rubbing it in. "We should go in the evening, right after the lamps go on. I bet you we'll find the next clue then."

River and I exchanged glances while Raiden beamed like his mate was the greatest thing to hit the Earth. In that moment, she truly was. Everything Mel said made sense, and the certainty in her voice got me excited for the next clue.

One more page.

One step closer.

Almost there.

"Mel, you riddle-solving master!" I squealed. "I could kiss you right now!"

She winked at me, her feline grin spreading. "Careful, witch. I might like it."

We took the hiking trails to get to the church. Not to cut down time, even though they were the shorter distance from where we were, but to keep ourselves hidden. No one knew what to expect when we got there, though I had an inkling that we might have another fae encounter on our hands. In all the ancient stories, there were four originals on Earth, and four pieces of the puzzle. It fit too well together.

I counted my steps as we walked, while River's fingers grazed mine every so often. Mel and Raiden led the way a few steps ahead, and I could sense their excitement cutting through my nerves. I felt awful for not telling Peyton about this, considering how close the church was to her house, but after Malakai and Illyria, any added life was a liability. I couldn't handle someone getting hurt on my watch. I also couldn't handle someone hurting the fae if one was waiting for us. There was a good chance they were here against their will, much like Malakai.

"Everyone ready for this?" I asked, as the cross atop the church appeared over the treeline.

Quietly we tiptoed through the church's empty parking lot and skirted around the side, following the path of the shadow cast by the colossal cross. With the bright light of the street-lamps behind us, the shadow looked like an arrow pointing in the direction we must go. *Here we go,* I thought and closed the distance between myself and the tip of the cross.

Nothing happened.

I looked around the group, then down to the spot where the cross's shadow skimmed the ground and waited. And waited. And waited.

River surveyed the vast open space we stood in. Trees rose high on all sides of us, concealing us from the town's view. This place was so private it was almost cozy, like we could stay awhile and relax.

"I don't get it!" Mel shrieked. "It was supposed to be right here! I was right, I know I was."

My spa-like serenity flew out the window. "Let me try my magic," I suggested, and started to call on the shadows. I froze. "Wait! Why did he mention the windmill?"

"I don't know. Because it's an obvious point of reference?"

"Maybe," I whispered. "But he said it twice. *The wind at your back.*"

I faced the direction of the cross's shadow, then turned around. My eyes traveled all the way up the church to the small round window at the apex of the roof. Briskly, my hand reached into my bag and I pulled out a velvet bag full of crystals. After the last two stops we made on this journey, I wasn't taking any chances; I needed all the magic I could get my hands on. My fingers grazed an amethyst point, and I laser-focused on the window, reaching deep inside to summon my air magic. A gust of wind blew past my ear. I aimed the magic toward it, taking control. I felt the wind surround me instantly. My hair whipped around my face and the muffled shouts of River and our friends died away in the whooshing sound filling my ears. Concentrating the wind into a powerful cylinder, I blasted it upward. It hit the thin pane of the stained glass and a small crack appeared between two bright red roses. I pushed further, the crack growing across the window.

"Billie, what are you doing?" River yelled from behind me.

Staying silent, I forced more wind into the glass until I heard a loud crack and it shattered before my eyes. Sharp pieces crumbled every which way, and I wiped the sweat off my brow, concentrating on the window and the pair of aquamarine eyes staring back at me. "Air fae," I said. "We have to get up there!" The others must have been in shock because nobody moved. "Now!" I screamed, and took off toward the back door of the church. I tested the door handle, finding it locked.

"How do you plan to get in there?" River asked.

"Step aside, kids." Raiden pushed past us and wrapped his thick fingers around the handle, twisting. The handle crumbled under his strength, and Raiden slid the door open, a cocky smile on his face.

"You're strong, we get it," River said, and shoved the shifter out of the way.

As we entered the church, Raiden motioned to the front of the building and I nodded, watching him scurry away into the darkness to make certain we were alone. Less than a minute later, he popped up in front of me again, holding two thumbs up. I let go of my breath and gestured to the spiral staircase on our left. A thick chain dangled from one side and a handmade sign hung off it that read *Employees Only*. I ducked under the chain, my back stiff as I walked up the steps. Fear settled in my throat and I prayed to the Goddess that the fae waiting for us in the attic was a friendly.

My prayers fell on deaf ears.

When we reached the top landing, the door of the attic swung open and a strong wind slapped me right in the face. I sputtered, teetering backward. River caught me before I fell all the way down the stairs and took everyone down with me like a set of dominos.

"Thanks," I said, righting myself. "No one hurt it. It might not be a danger to us." A crashing sound penetrated the church, and I pressed my palms to my ears and dropped to the ground. "What was that?"

We looked around, then down the steps to see a giant chandelier lying in pieces on the floor below us. The fae must have used its air magic to tear it right off its hinges. "Are you crazy?" I yelled into the dark room. "You could have killed someone!"

"Pretty sure that was the idea," River said. He stepped around me to go inside the room and I tried to hold him back, but he was already halfway there. Wind surrounded him in a tornado. His body lifted off the ground, limbs flying every-where and nearly breaking. I rushed after him, summoning more air magic. My power collided with the fae's and it dropped its hold on River. His back slammed to the floor, and he gasped for air, rolling over to draw his knees into his chest while he struggled to breathe. My neck twisted to the shadow of a man appearing in the darkness. He was slender, and he clung to the corner of the room close to the broken window. The light peering through the shattered glass reflected off his aquamarine eyes and made them look like they were glowing. He had a pointed nose and a neck so long it seemed unnatural. Around it, a thick metal collar gleamed as he moved. In the center of the collar, a familiar symbol stared me dead in the face. The rune symbol for water.

I held my hands up, dropping my magic. "We're not here to hurt you," I said. "We want to help."

I pointed to the collar and turned my palm upward, freeing a few shadows to swirl atop it so the fae understood I had the power to free him.

It had the opposite effect.

As soon as my shadows appeared, the fae stepped out of the corner and closed in on me. The wind he controlled picked up, and I had to spread my feet wider to keep upright. My eyes watered and I held my ground, getting a better look at the man. Scars covered his entire neck; I looked down at his hand to the long claws on his fingers. *He tried to cut the collar off himself.* My head tilted back to the ceiling and bile rose in my chest when I saw the symbols carved there. They were thin enough that no one would notice if they made their way up here, but I knew what they were. Cathan made sure no human could ever see the fae, even if they stood right in front of him.

Tears flooded my vision, and I gasped for air as more wind blasted into my gaping mouth.

How long? How many years has this poor creature been trapped in the attic alone? His magic dwindling, his life force gone, all to guard another piece of the puzzle.

I wanted to cut Cathan's head off with a dull knife.

The fae moved to strike me and I lifted my hands higher to show him we didn't pose a threat, but he was too afraid to understand. His hands moved quickly, casting more of his magic toward me. I had to get out of the way, and fast.

"Get away from her!" Mal shouted, and I heard her steps pick up from behind me. The floorboards shook beneath us as she ran to interfere.

"Mel, NO!" I screamed, but it was too late.

The fae grabbed hold of her, hoisting her up in the air like a rag doll. Her body twisted and turned as the fae pushed more of his magic out to surround her. She tried to get free, and fur appeared along her arms and legs—the lion inside breaking loose.

Winds pummeled her body and raised her higher at an increasing speed. Her head hit the ceiling and my knees knocked from the sound. Behind me, a wild roar sounded as I spun around to watch Raiden's lion charging for the fae.

Then two things happened at the same time.

The fae threw his arms to the side, and the current he manifested tossed Mel toward the broken window, right through what was left of the glass. As he did so, Raiden's lion crashed into him and sank his sharp teeth into the fae's throat. Around the metal collar and through, right to the bone. I heard a loud snap, and the fae's eyes dimmed and closed. His hands dropped to the side, his magic evaporating. A loud thud filled the room, and I froze, my blood running cold. Raiden roared again and his pain spread through me. I ran to the window, River on my heels, and as we looked down, my heart shattered. There on the ground, right next to the church, lay Mel. Her left arm bent at an unnatural angle and her eyes were wide open, devoid of all life.

Chapter Fifteen

Logan

The fire fae continued to attack from across the small pond as I readied my defenses. Despite the fact that there were only two of them, the bloody bastards sure knew how to cause some damage. Their magic rushed to the surface, and they pushed out streams of fire from their fingers that reshaped as it hit the ground. The fire thickened, clinging to itself to reform into a hot, sticky mess. My eyes narrowed. Lava. Fabulous. The pricks were going to destroy the entire forest at this rate. The lava spread over the Earth and rolled in like molasses, picking up speed as the fire idiots worked their magic. There was enough of it to fill a pickup truck—plenty to destroy the pond and any life in it. Sweat soaked through my trousers from the gathering heat. I looked down at the stain forming and grimaced. *Great, now it looks like I bloody pissed myself.*

My gaze flickered to the two tossers at the edge of the pond and I cursed under my breath. The last thing we needed was for the fae to start their childish war games, but it seemed that these idiots didn't get the memo. Their scar-covered arms stretched outward, directing the lava closer to the pond where a young water fae sat defenseless. I checked the water, realizing quickly that she was completely alone. Her loud hisses filled the forest, and I rolled up my sleeves, calling for my magic.

The shadows shot out and rushed over the water toward the angry-looking bastards standing there.

One fae looked up, her blood-red eyes zeroing in on the shadows. Without looking my way, she elbowed the grizzly looking fae beside her and nodded to my magic. If the fae was afraid, he didn't show it. His arms continued to direct the lava at the pond, and I caught the slightest curl of his lips as steam rose from the water.

The morons were trying to boil the water fae in her own home.

Chest rising, I stepped into the pond, careful not to draw attention to myself. Having the fire fae acting up was one thing, but I definitely did not want the fishes getting upset. I scanned their scaly bodies, trying to see if I recognized someone that might see some reason. I did not. Deflated, I let my palms graze the cool surface of the pond and pushed the shadows into it. They spread and swirled, mixing with the liquid until I stood in complete darkness. Small waves flowed from behind me as Savannah treaded to my side.

Her face reflected my thoughts to a tee. This was a bloody cock-up.

I pushed on. The shadows crept to the edge of the pond, and this time when the fire fae commanded the lava further into the water, it hissed and smoked, the heat in it dying away. The male growled and looked over at the water fae, finally acknowledging my existence. I growled back. *I got bite too, you daft punk.*

"Logan," Savannah warned a little too late.

While I was concentrating on the man, his partner in crime managed to sneak by to stand behind Savannah and me. Her eyes burned into the back of my neck, and I turned around in time to see her form a fireball and toss it straight toward me. I dove out of the way, taking Savannah down into the water with me. Coldness splashed around us. I watched as the pond rose into a massive wall, obscuring us from our attacker.

My head twisted to the water fae commanding the magic, and I nodded a *thank you*, focusing my attention back on the man. The water wall hissed at our backs as the wild woman continued to barrel fireball after fireball at it.

I shook my head. *The definition of insanity.*

Without much finesse, I shoved all my magic out of my body and threw it at the man nearing the pond. He must have not anticipated the clumsy attack because when my shadows collided with his chest, his eyes bulged and all the air in his lungs escaped. His muscled arms swung in front as my magic propelled him backward, away from the water and into the dense forest. I heard a yelp followed by a thud, then another. The fae hit something hard and dropped like a sack of dirt.

Another cry sounded nearby, as the woman rushed off to find him.

I turned to the water fae. "Care to tell me what that was about, bird?" I asked.

She shrugged and turned away, dipping low into the water. Eyes widening, I creased my brow and looked at Savannah. Was this woman actually bloody *leaving* after we saved her arse? As the girl's long, matted hair sank further out of sight, I felt my body stiffen. I was pretty used to being disrespected by the fire fae of this realm, but this was a new low. Waverly once told me not to take anything personally, yet standing here now, I knew in my gut that if I were Cathan, the water fae wouldn't dare walk away. Hell, if I were Cathan, we wouldn't even be standing here. The blood-thirsty plunker would have already thrown all three of them into the dungeons.

While I was picturing locking up the water fae, Savannah ducked into the water and disappeared before my eyes. Mere seconds later her head popped up, followed by her soaking body as she re-emerged, pulling the water fae behind her by her hair. The woman cursed and slashed at Savannah's arms with her long nails. If my girl felt any pain, I wouldn't have known it.

Teeth chattering, Savannah tossed the fae on the ground at my feet. "Talk."

"I was handling them," the girl said, nostrils flaring.

"I'm sure you were," I agreed. "Why were they after you?"

She shook her head, and her sea-green eyes grew twice in size. "Not me. The male."

I wasn't sure if she was acting dense on purpose or if this was a water fae trait I hadn't discovered yet. If it was, I truly despised it. While there wasn't many male water fae around, I had to guess there were more than one, and the girl's answer made my head hurt from annoyance. I rubbed my temples and asked, "Which male?"

"The witch lover."

Of course. Of bloody course. Heaven forbid there'd be an issue in this slimy realm and one of ours wouldn't be right at the center. I wasn't sure why the fire fae were after Solen, but I was going to get some answers, even if I had to drag this girl to the palace and interrogate her Cathan-style.

Shadows crept out of my fingers and wrapped around my legs and waist. I noticed the girl's eyes dart to them, her face blanching. "What issue do they have with Solen?" I asked.

"The deadly kind."

Beside me, Savannah rolled her eyes, and I swore I could hear it. Getting the fae to talk was like pulling teeth, and I was sure even that would've been a smoother process. My eyes locked on the girl and I let out a low growl.

She shivered. "They think if they get rid of Solen, they'll sever your connection to the witch on Earth."

"Billie?" Savannah asked.

The girl nodded. "They also think it'll make it impossible for you to open the portal. They do not want to leave here."

"But Solen is not the one that's trying to open it," Savannah said.

Realization dawned on me before the fae had a chance to explain. I glanced from her to Savannah. "Victoria," I said. "All that new magic she'd been using. It must be from Solen."

"The male is teaching her the ways of our land," the fae whispered. "She is a natural at working the realm's energies. Her abilities have earned her enemies among my kind. You must understand, a witch taking what is ours opens old wounds, ones some have never forgotten. Or forgiven."

I let the shadows go, and they crawled back inside the confines of my body. "I'm sorry they feel that way," I said, and meant it. "But Billie and Victoria are nothing like the witches your kind knew all those years ago. They are not with the High Coven. And they're trying to save a lot of people."

"Like a LOT!" Savannah repeated.

The girl didn't look too impressed, though that could have been the water fae in her coming through. In all the time I'd spent here, the water fae did not much care for anything that didn't affect them directly. They were outsiders in their own realm and liked it that way. I understood their stance. It wasn't that long ago that I had the same mentality. My eyes locked on Savannah. Until her.

"No matter what some think, Solen is helping a good cause," I said.

"You don't understand," the girl rebutted. "Solen's power —it isn't like the rest of us. What he is teaching the witch is not to be passed on to anyone but the fae. She is not fae."

I arched a brow. "What do you mean, his powers are not like the rest of yours?"

"Solen is special. He doesn't use the energy of Faerie. He creates it."

"You mean—"

"Your witch can make magic out of thin air. Thanks to Solen."

Uh-oh. That sounded like an ability others would definitely kill for. Especially the fire fae, who were as obvious as ever about wanting to be in control of Faerie. But something didn't make sense to me. I wasn't buying that the fire fae were after Solen to avoid leaving the realm. And how did they even know about Billie's plan? I looked around. This place was worse than a high school cafeteria when it came to gossip.

I took a step closer to the girl. "This magic Solen taught Victoria—could she teach it to others if she was forced to?"

"I don't see why not."

"What are you thinking?" Savannah asked, her voice laced with concern.

My head swiveled from the pond to the regions beyond the cliffs where the fire fae resided. The two we got rid of were a long way from home and heading farther into the forest. There was only one thing in the trees that would interest them, and I hated how long it took me to realize it. I swallowed the lump in my throat. "We have to go, love," I told Savannah. "Victoria is in trouble."

As we picked up pace and tore into the forest, I prayed we weren't too late.

Chapter Sixteen

Billie

The resistance house was silent and melancholy and full of shadows. I sat on the porch steps, my bare feet grazing the dirt below, and watched the trees. It had been a few hours since the shifters left to bury Mel's body, and I was starting to wonder if they were planning to return. Though I could feel River through our bond, he stayed silent. I respected the distance he needed—the distance they all needed—today. Mel was a big part of everyone's lives here, but she was a mother figure to most of the young shifters. Losing her felt like losing a piece of your soul.

A loud roar sounded in the far distance, followed by yelps and howls. Birds took off from the treetops and circled above before dispersing.

It had begun.

I looked down at my lap and at the book I held. Wiping the tears away with the back of my hand, I focused my eyes on the script, reading it under my breath:

"If you are haunted by the past,
Know death is never meant to last.
For in the final resting place
The ones who hunt will give no chase.
On that grave day cradled in Furs,
You'll finally find that which is yours."

I slammed the book shut and tossed it onto the deck with a sigh. Either I was getting dumber, or the riddles were getting tougher; whatever the reason, my brain refused to even attempt solving the next clue. I blamed the day. After we said our goodbyes to Mel, the shifters took over while the rest of us stayed behind. I wanted to go with them and pay my respects, but River convinced me otherwise. This was shifter territory, and they needed to do this alone. Though I understood it, I hated being left behind.

Mel was important to me, too.

I looked at the book. She was gone because of my asswipe of a father.

"They'll be back soon."

I turned to the sound of a bell-like voice. "Hi, Lorelei," I said. "What happens after?"

The reaper's violet eyes dimmed, and she walked past me, took the steps down to the landing, and cast a watchful gaze on the tree line. "There will be a remembrance dinner this evening, followed by what I can only describe as an all-night party. The shifters do not believe in mourning as much as they do in celebrating."

"Will Raiden be there?" I asked. I couldn't imagine partying if I lost River, but the shifters had their own set of beliefs.

Lorelei nodded. "He will. Though I assume he will probably leave right after."

"Leave?"

"Losing a mate is no light matter," Lorelei explained. "Raiden will require time and space from all things which once included Melody. I'm afraid that means this house and everyone in it."

I blinked rapidly. "When will he be back?"

The reaper shrugged. "When he is ready." She looked down at the book, her chin tipping toward it. "Still no luck, I presume?"

"Nope. My brain is mush right now."

A smile tugged at the corners of Lorelei's thin lips. She turned back to the trees, her long hair blowing in the wind as she said, "Perhaps they can help."

My stomach tensed as I followed her gaze to the oncoming group. Bells rang in the distance, and the smell of mixed herbs wafted up my nostrils. My magic hummed beneath the surface of my skin as the rogue witches approached with Catarina at the helm. I raised my hand to wave, then lowered it. Shock rang through me at the sight of a familiar head of hair. Theodora's bright blue locks were coiffed so high atop her head, she looked like a blue beacon. The feather-covered turquoise overcoat she wore didn't help the visual. Beside the high priestess, my mother walked triumphantly, and when my eyes found hers, she winked. Right behind her and Theodora, a few younger coven witches approached with stacks of books in their hands. If I didn't know better, I'd have thought all these women were part of the same coven.

Catarina was the first to climb the porch steps. "We hear you might need some assistance with a riddle," she said.

"How did you...?" I found my mother again. "I guess you told them?"

Beatrix nodded and smiled. "All hands on deck."

I smiled and reached for the Book of Darkness, but my fingers landed on an empty spot on the deck. Scanning the witches, I spotted it in Theodora's hands, her fingers clasping the edge as she inspected the paper. I cleared my throat, and she looked up, startled. "It's unbelievable that no one ever found this before."

"No one had Cathan's blood before," I reminded her.

"Right, of course," the high priestess said. "I see the old fool is better at hiding pages than he is at writing riddles."

My ears burned. "What do you mean?"

"Oh, you must be kidding? Do you truly mean to tell me that after all the Indiana Jones movies we watched, you can't figure this out?"

I cringed, remembering my excitement at spending an evening binge watching those films with Theodora. She had the biggest crush on Harrison Ford, and I... well, I wasn't sure what my reason was. All I knew was that I loved spending time with her. Something about her excitement made me come alive. Theodora was different back then, more at ease with herself. Granted, that was before I became Sebyl's number one enemy. And definitely before I mated with a shadower.

Life sure changed a lot.

I raised one eyebrow at Theodora. "What have you got?"

"The witch cemetery in Carriage Hill," she answered. "Obviously."

"Why *obviously*?" Catarina asked. The venom in her voice implied that she either wished she was the one to solve the riddle, or that this was a huge waste of her precious time. It was hard to tell, since she was almost always short with people.

Theodora grinned sweetly. "The original witches believed that if their magic passed on, they would live on. That covers the *death and past* portions of the riddle. Then there's those who hunt."

"The witch hunters," my mother said.

"Bingo!" Theodora exclaimed. "No point chasing dead witches, so they wouldn't be at the cemetery."

It was a crude explanation, but Theodora was definitely on the right track. Perhaps all those movies really did make her a riddle mastermind. I bet Cathan didn't expect that when he wrote the damn thing. I came to stand beside her and looked at the riddle over her shoulder. "What about the last two lines? What furs would there be at the cemetery? Shifters?"

"There wouldn't be furs there," Catarina said. "But there would be *firs*. I bet you that's why this particular word is capitalized, because it's meant to deceive."

"Fir trees," I said. I picked up my phone and sent out two identical messages, one to River and one to Peyton. *'We're looking for fir trees at the witch cemetery. I'll see you both at the house. This is our final stop.'*

Being unable to hold my excitement, I reread the riddle, bouncing from heel to heel. This was it. One more stop, one more piece of the puzzle, and we'd have our answer. I wasn't sure what the outcome would be, but I hoped it would either help us stop the bomb or give us some idea as to how to open the portal so I can force Cathan's hand. One way or another, we were almost there. We were going to save everyone.

I let my grin spread wide and linger, calmness settling over my body.

If I bothered to look further, I would have realized that it wasn't calm as much as it was nerves. I had much to be nervous about; I just didn't know it yet.

Chapter
Seventeen

River

"Down!" Catarina yelled out behind me.

She reached a hand into the flowing layers of skirt she wore and dug out a pouch of crystals, readying to attack.

My body reacted on instinct and I hit the ground, my nose digging into the dirt. Above me, a whooshing sound passed, and I looked around the edge of the gravestone I lay next to as a massive ball of fire exploded on a nearby tree. The bark singed and hissed; the tree swayed but surprisingly stayed upright. I jerked my head back and growled at the fire fae that launched the attack. His thick horns pointed to the dusk-colored sky and his expression fermented. I got ready to stand and froze.

From behind the fae, the jingle of a crystal-lined skirt filled my ears as Catarina ran full force toward my attacker. Her hands moved fast, tearing pieces off the necklace she wore as she grasped for crystals and herbs to aid her magic. The fae heard her coming only a moment too late.

His bright orange eyes widened as the rogue witch

flipped her palms and shot her own brand of fire magic directly into his chest. It was so quick he didn't have time to duck. The fire collided with his rock-hard body and sent him flying backward, his breath leaving a trail behind him as he flew.

The entire spectacle played out like a movie scene, and if I wasn't so used to this being my life now, I would have been shocked. Instead, I pushed myself to my knees and glanced at the gravestone. Marie Duchamp. Dead for over four hundred years, from the looks of the etching on the stone. I brushed dirt off my face and cringed, pieces of Marie's final resting place falling away from my skin. Bones aching, I scanned the cemetery for signs of Billie, finding her not far from where I crouched. Sweat beaded off her forehead and her hair was a matted mess as she blasted her shadows in all directions. Around her, the fire fae ran in circles, trying to best my girl while avoiding the hits of her magic. My thighs tightened as I jumped up and ran to her.

The closer I got, the faster I realized Billie did not need me.

She twirled around and threw more of her shadows out, sending them straight for two fae on her left. The shadows pieced out into dozens of dark ribbons, each swirling outward to surround the fae. The assholes had the audacity to chuckle, thinking they actually stood a chance against her, no doubt.

They sure as hell didn't.

While the shadows swarmed around them, Billie was already readying another attack. Her hand reached into a pocket and something glimmered in the setting sunlight before she fisted her hands. A crystal. I looked at her face and smiled as I watched her eyes lose all color. A bright light shone from within them, and her lips pursed in concentration as she willed the elements into existence. It had been a while since I'd seen my girl's eyes glow, and I knew that only meant one thing.

The bastards were about to get it bad.

Billie's fists sparked and flames engulfed them. She brought both hands to her lips and blew out a wind strong enough to topple houses, aiming the flames at the fae. Her fire magic pierced through the shadows surrounding the two men and filled the ball of darkness she created. Screams rose from within the black bubble of shadow magic. I watched in awe as Billie torched our attackers like they were marshmallows on a stick. A second later, she dropped her arms, and the shadows dispersed, the fire dying away with them. Steam rose off the two bastards inside and they dropped like sacks of garbage to the ground. Fighting fire with fire seemed to work fine when it came to the fire fae.

I waited for a moment until I saw the fae's chests rise up and down, indicating they were alive.

It seemed Billie was checking on the same thing, and when she was satisfied that she didn't kill the pricks, she turned on her heels and ran farther into the graveyard, where Theodora and Beatrix took on five more fire fae. I wasn't sure why my girl was so adamant on making sure the idiots that attacked us as soon as we stepped foot in the witch cemetery weren't harmed. If it were up to me, they'd all be dead already. But it wasn't up to me, it never was.

Shaking my head clear of heated thoughts, I started after Billie.

I didn't even clear a foot forward.

Something hard and large slammed into my back and I toppled over, face planting into Miss Duchamp again. If zombies were real, I was pretty sure Marie would have her cold, dead witch fingers around my throat for disturbing her peace two times over. My teeth gritted together and I spat out grave-dirt that dug itself under my tongue. Whatever crashed into me was now putting all its weight onto my back and pressing me farther into the ground. I yanked my head back and gasped for breath, but was shoved down again, my mouth crashing into the earth. Fingers pressed into the sides of my skull and held me down while I struggled to breathe. My muscles tensed. *I've had it with the fae.*

Palms pushing down, I held myself steady and called for the wolf. *Time to play, buddy.*

It took him no time to respond and I felt my body morph and shift to let the wolf come through. My bones cracked, arms and legs snapping into unnatural positions with the damn fire fae on my back like a fucking leech. My upper body shot up, and I heard a grunt as the fae got knocked off kilter and slid off me to the ground. The pain of shifting into wolf form was like a tickle I barely registered. I twisted around, my tail swinging behind me, and buried my paws down to get a better grip. Before me, the fae that had me pinned was looking less and less confident as he took in my wolf form.

Sure, the bastard was big—and ugly as sin—but I had one thing he didn't. Damn huge teeth and the desire to use them.

I lunged forward, my paws stamping into the fae's chest to hold him down. When the fae's back hit the earth, I pumped down on his chest a second time, then a third, just to get my point across. The fae's body sank into the soft ground, his pointed ears filling with dirt. *Two can play this game, you lizard-looking moron!*

Unhinging my jaw, I loosened a breath and rushed my

teeth toward the fae's throat, stopping an inch above his skin. *No killing,* I reminded myself. My breath billowed through my nostrils and the wolf's hungry saliva dripped down, coating the fae's throat. Marking him. I shook my mane and howled, then hopped off the fae to stand beside him. The blubbering fool scrambled to his feet, confusion coating his features. It took him a minute to sober up, and then he was jumping for me again like a madman. Which was exactly what I expected him to do.

I stood motionless, watching him get closer, closer, my back paw tapping the drop-off in the ground behind me that led to an unfilled grave. When the fae was mere inches from me, I jutted to the side and watched amusingly as he toppled over the edge and fell face first into the six-foot hole. Before he had a chance to climb his giant ass out, I kicked my hind legs out and hit the tombstone that stood next to the plot. It swayed back and forth, trying to regain balance, then shot downward. I heard a yelp followed by a thud, then silence. Edging closer to the open hole, I peered down and tilted my head to inspect the unconscious fae trapped under the stone at the bottom of the grave. His large nostrils flared as he breathed, and I could tell it would be a while before he came to. I glanced at Marie's grave next to him. *Enjoy the company.*

Behind the copse of trees that hid the graveyard from the world, screaming ensued. My legs hit the ground running, and I picked up speed until I made my way through the thick row of pines to the opposite side.

I smelled the smoke before I saw the fire.

One—I'm not sure which—fae decided to play arsonist and set the entire line of trees ablaze. At this time of year, with the leaves gone and the branches dry and ready for winter, all it probably took was one spark. I growled deep in my throat and ducked down low, avoiding inhaling any more of the smoke that rose through the graveyard. My eyes watered and the wolf's heightened sense of smell made me want to gag. The fire smelled like rot and death, and I didn't even want to think about what that could mean, considering where we were.

Crawling, I inched to where I felt Billie's presence and was relieved to find her unharmed. Her eyes had gone back to their natural blue, and she somehow managed to find time to tie the unruly mess that was her hair into a high bun. Her arms stretched out, and I followed them to see her holding hands with Theodora and Luna. The high priestesses chanted in a language I didn't understand, the same phrase over and over. Between them, Billie swayed from side to side, as she often did when getting ready to cast. Their combined magic was overwhelming, and I could feel it smooth my fur down as it passed. Something wet hit my ears and I let out a low whine, gazing at the sky. Above me, furious clouds gathered seconds before rain poured down on all of us.

The flames fizzled out and the three women dropped their hold on each other. Billie cracked her neck and stared down at one fae that I assumed was to blame for almost destroying the entire cemetery.

"You asked for it now," she said.

In one swift move, she kicked her boot behind her and grabbed her dagger as it flew in the air. Her eyes sparked with thundering anger as she ran toward the fae, who now crouched on the ground like a complete loser. He had every reason to be afraid. When Billie got this way, there was no telling what fury she was going to unleash.

I sat back in the mud and watched while she closed the

distance between her and the fae. Suddenly, something caught my attention.

Tied to the fae's leather belt, was a small packet. It looked entirely uninteresting except for one small fact: the fire rune carved into its center. I howled to get Billie's attention, but she couldn't hear me from all the commotion. *"Babe, stop!"* I warned through our bond.

Billie flashed me a quick glance, but kept moving.

Oh, for the love of.... I shifted faster than I have in my entire time of having my abilities. Not bothering to find clothes, I took off after Billie. Running was... not great.

"STOP!" I roared.

Luckily, before any more of my parts got knocked around, Billie halted and looked at me. Her head tilted to the side, and she creased her eyebrows, giving me a questioning look. *Freaking finally.* I pointed to the satchel. "He has a piece of the book."

The fae started to crab-crawl away, but Billie was faster. She lifted her leg and slammed a boot into his throat, saying, "Don't even think about it." The fae sucked in breaths between fits of coughing. When the bastard stopped moving, she reached into his satchel and pulled out a familiar-looking piece of parchment.

Kneeling, Billie flattened the paper. "Mom!" she called out. "Get the book!"

As if on cue, Beatrix all but manifested at our side. Her eyes briefly took in my unclothed form and while a smile tugged at her lips, I was grateful she didn't comment. Instead, she reached into her backpack and pulled out the Book of Darkness, laying it out on the ground by the parchment. Billie's cheeks puffed out as she tried to fit the piece into place, but it didn't work. There was no sparkling magic, no fusing of the paper, no annoying little riddle showing up to move us forward. It was as though the parchment we found was not a part of Cathan's pathetic game at all.

Billie's aggravation cut through me. She turned to the fae, fuming. "What the hell is this? Why isn't it working?"

The fae shook his head. "I don't know what it is," he answered. "My instructions were to hold it for the king in case he should ever come looking for it."

"Your king is gone," Billie said. She looked up at me, her eyes watering. "It didn't work."

Settling down beside her, I pulled her into me and pressed a soft kiss to her forehead. "Let me see this thing."

Hands trembling, Billie passed the parchment to me and I looked it over. It was no different from the other we found except for the size. It was much smaller. Carefully, I laid it on the other page in the book that was covered in riddles. It fit, but only half way. Sucking in a quick breath, I said, "I think we're missing the other half of this."

"What do you mean?" Beatrix asked.

I pointed to the right edge of the paper. "This part fits what we have, but this edge here," I ran my finger along the torn side of the parchment, "it was ripped off. In a hurry, from the looks of it."

"But why—"

I held my hand up, silencing Billie. My eyes narrowed as I brought the paper up, the light of the setting sun shining through it. It was so light I could barely make out the writing, yet it was there all the same. One word, etched into the bottom corner of the parchment. "Home," I read aloud.

"Home?" Billie asked. "Where is home?"

"Faerie," Beatrix answered right as I let out a string of words I wouldn't want school children hearing. "He left the other piece in Faerie. It's the only place Cathan would ever consider being his home."

"Are you saying what I think you're saying?" I asked, panic settling over me.

The tears Billie tried to hold back ran freely down her face and when she spoke, she looked into the distance towards where the portal to Faerie once stood. "If we want to stop the bomb, we need the piece from Faerie. And we need to open the portal. We can't unite the pages otherwise."

"But we don't know how!" I exclaimed.

She nodded. "And Cathan knew it would come to that. He knew, and he set us up. No matter how we played the game, we always ended up in the same place."

"What place is that?" Beatrix asked.

Darkness filled Billie's eyes, and if I hadn't seen her shine so brightly before, I would have sworn she was made of nothing but nightmares. Her hands fisted at her sides, she ground her teeth together so loud, it made the earth shake under us. "We have to release him if we stand any chance of saving this world."

Chapter Eighteen

Billie

I didn't stop shaking until we reached the townhouse, though I wasn't sure if it was from fear or anger. Somehow, in the midst of all the riddle chasing, I actually let myself believe that we could one-up Cathan. I should have known better. There was no out-tricking a trickster.

The lane of townhouses came into view and my stomach pitched violently. A few more minutes and we'd be right where Cathan wanted us.

I didn't know if this was exactly what my sad excuse for a father had in mind when he set up the riddles—after all, no one could have that much foresight—but I knew he planted the clues knowing they led to a dead end. I also knew that considering how long the riddle pages have been on Earth, he'd been planning this for a long while. Likely longer than I've been alive and even well before he met Mom.

For a second, I wondered if Cathan ever cared about me at all. When I first met him, he sure pretended to be pleased to have a successor to his name, but that was all a lie. My father was a self-fulfilling, righteous monster who only worked to serve his own needs. In the past, I knew exactly what those needs were. Now... well, I had no idea why he went to these dramatic extremes and set up a freaking treasure hunt.

I shook off the thoughts.

Whatever Cathan wanted, we were about to find out.

The house was quieter than usual, and I shifted my weight to the tips of my toes as we walked down the main hallway toward the library stairs. Theodora took the helm of our procession, leading us down the spiral staircase like rats after a song. Knots formed in my gut with every step closer to what I knew would be our doom. Despite everyone trying to convince me that we had it under control and there was no way Cathan would be able to escape again, I had my doubts. But then I thought about what River told me on the way here —we're going to die in a few days anyway, might as well try.

My eyes burned, and I tightened my grip on River's hand, staring at my mother's hair bobbing as she walked. I should have called Peyton to come tonight, and I should have stopped by the Chandlers' on the way here. There was so little time I didn't even think about what it could mean if we couldn't convince Cathan to thwart his plans. I wouldn't have a chance to say goodbye to those I loved.

"Ready?" River asked.

I looked down, realizing for the first time that my feet were planted in the center of the High Coven library. In front of me, taunting, stood the round mahogany table and upon it lay the jar holding the man I hated most in the world. "As ready as I'll ever be," I said.

He kissed the back of my neck and took a step backward, leaving me to face Cathan. The other four witches secured spots around the table, and I looked up at my mother's reassuring smile. I didn't even bother smiling back when I said, "Let's get it over with."

The women clutched hands as I took my position. Feet steady on the wood floor, I pulled the jar closer and wrapped my fingers around the lid. Before I could chicken out, I twisted it open and placed the jar on the table. The dark shadows that made up Cathan rushed from the jar and into the room. My body responded instantly, my own shadows releasing until the entire library was so dark, I couldn't see a foot in front of me.

"Now!" I yelled out.

On my command, my mother and the others called forth their air magic and a bright light filled the room. I directed my shadows around Cathan's, throwing my energy out in chunks to entwine with his. At first, nothing happened. Then, little by little, I saw a shape begin to form in the darkness. An arm, a leg, a torso. All of them were transparent and creepy as hell. I looked at my mother, wondering if this was how she saw Cathan the first time she met him when he was unable to fully form in our realm. Beatrix was way too busy holding onto the light to pay attention to me, so I focused all my energy on the wicked fae coming to life on the library table.

Cathan's body went from vapor to fluid to solid in mere moments. One second he was nothing but smoke, and the next his feet were as deeply rooted on the tabletop as mine were on the floor. Thank the Goddess his clothes manifested with him because I didn't think I could handle seeing that right now. Or ever.

I grabbed my mother's hand on one side and Catarina's on the other and joined my air power with theirs. The light that filled the room whooshed past us and swarmed the circle we formed. In unison, we raised our arms, and the light followed, surrounding Cathan in a bright wall. It continued to crawl upward until the man that called himself my father was entombed in a dome of light so bright it was blinding.

As Cathan's awareness returned to him, he smashed his body against the light, and I heard a hiss leave his lips; his shadow magic reacting to our magic and shrinking away. His blue eyes knifed to mine. "Let me guess," he said with a smirk. "You made it as far as the graveyard."

I wanted to know better. I wanted to not fall for his crap and keep my cool. I wanted to show him that I wasn't bothered by his bullshit games and his disgusting want to destroy everyone I loved.

What I wanted and what I did were in direct opposition.

Before anyone could stop me, I grabbed hold of my dagger and flipped it to face Cathan. Then I lunged for his jugular.

Chapter Nineteen

Savannah

aerie's forest burned.

I blinked rapidly and held my palm over my mouth to keep from breathing in smoke. With my other hand, I pulled up the bow, trembling. Sucking in a deep breath and holding it, I nocked an arrow and let it fly. It hit the fire fae in my sightline in the leg and she screamed out in pain, dropping her hold on Victoria.

"Nice shot!" the witch hollered, her hands already busy working her magic.

I rolled my eyes. I was aiming for the fae's shoulder, so it was actually an abysmal shot, but whatever got the job done at this point.

By the time we finally reached Waverly's settlement, the fire fae had taken control. Fire spread through the trees, destroying everything in sight. There were twenty of them, give or take, and they were on a mission to kill anyone in their way as long as it got them to Victoria. As Logan and I rushed to the rescue, my head and gut were in opposition. I wanted to subdue the idiots who thought they could manhandle their way to get what they wanted; I also wanted to see them bleed.

Near to me, Logan used his shadows to put out whatever fire he could while Solen helped pull people out of the rumble and to safety. My chest heaved as I watched him hoist two crying fae children over his shoulders and run into the foliage that was left unscathed. When Solen put them down, he said something I couldn't hear, and the kids took off into the forest like spooked deer. My gaze traveled over the expense of the village as I took in the destruction.

Almost every treehouse was gone, and those that weren't would not hold up much longer. I was sure there were fae inside some of them that would not have the same luck as the kids had. My eyes locked on a fire fae on the left. His entire body was engulfed in flame and as he stalked through the village, sparks flew off him, catching on branches and lighting them up. The fire fae didn't even notice—nor care—for the chaos he was leaving behind. His attention was elsewhere.

I turned my head.

Victoria.

The witch stood about twenty feet from the creepy pyromaniac heading her way, her brow furrowed in concentration. With arms out in front of her, she held a wall of intertwining tree roots that jutted out of Faerie's purple Earth. I wondered when the hell she had time to create the barrier; I saw her scramble away literally moments ago. Victoria's lips tightened, and she poured more of her magic into the wall. In response, more roots shot out from the ground and intertwined with the others, spreading around the village to form a shield. On the opposite side, incoherent shouts rose as a few fire fae worked to bring her wall down. Their blows pounded at the roots, but Victoria's magic held strong. Her feet skidded across the Earth and she leaned her body forward, pushing to hold the fae at bay.

Her back to the danger approaching her, the witch had no way of seeing the monster coming up behind her.

"Incoming!" I yelled out.

I sprinted toward Victoria with my bow at the ready. When I was squarely between her and the fire fae, I twirled on my heels and loosed an arrow. It pierced the air and impaled itself directly in the fae's right bicep. His arm shot back and his body whirled around, losing balance. Instead of running away like I hoped he would, the fae gripped one end of the arrow lodged in his arm and snapped the shaft, tossing the fletching to the ground. Teeth grinding together, he reached around the back and pulled the arrow out in one fell swoop. Then his attention was on me.

The bastard charged for me like a bull, dust kicking up behind him as he ran. My fingers grazed another arrow, and I worked to get it in place, but I was running out of time. The distance between us grew smaller and smaller. Sweat beaded on the back of my neck, and though I had very little skill in hand-to-hand combat, I tossed the bow and readied to take the fae on.

He was so close, I could smell him. Smoke and sweat and tar. A disgusting combination.

The fae inched toward me and time seemed to slow. I brought my fists up, though I wasn't sure what I was expecting to accomplish. This guy was ten times bigger than me and could probably rip my head off with his nasty little teeth. It didn't matter; I had to do something.

"Let's do this," I hissed out.

But nothing happened.

The fire fae never reached me. His body froze mid-leap, and I watched his eyes widen until they looked like they might pop right the hell out. The fae's feet raised up from the ground and for a second, I thought the asswipe learned how to levitate. He didn't. My jaw slacked and for the first time, I noticed Logan's shadows around the fae's chest and waist. They hoisted him up into the air and held him for a second before launching him higher. I shielded my eyes from the sunlight, looking up at the fae as the shadows vanished. The fae froze in space for a moment, then tumbled down as gravity took hold.

I looked away right as he hit the ground. Slowly, I found Logan, his shadows rolling like waves back into his body. "What happened to no casualties?" I asked, repeating his words back to him.

He grimaced. "That one had it coming. Help Victoria!"

Logan swung around and blasted more of his shadows into the trees to buy Solen time to rescue whoever was left behind. There was so much screaming, I thought my ears would bleed. This was worse than the time Morgan convinced us to go to some underground club full of losers with questionable music taste and way too many speakers. I couldn't hear out of my left ear for weeks.

A loud boom shook the forest as a massive tree toppled and crashed into the Earth.

So much worse.

A loose spark hit my arm and the hair on it singed and burned. I swatted at the red spot, turning around to find Victoria take on two fire fae like a badass. She moved fluidly from side to side, avoiding the fireballs the bastards threw at her expertly. Her time with Solen must have involved more than magic training, because I did not remember the witch having these moves. My jaw gaped as Victoria took off in a sprint and lunged herself off a tree trunk to fly high in the air. She wrapped an arm around the neck of one fae while using all the force of her legs to kick the one standing next to him. The fae catapulted backward, losing his balance and quickly falling down like a sack of crap. All the while, Victoria swung around the fae she held and pushed her free palm to his rigid back. A flash surrounded her hand, and I saw the fae's eyes roll back into his skull. He went down harder than his friend.

As Victoria dislodged herself from her victim, she shot me a quick wink.

Oh, my... do I have a lady crush on the witch?

I didn't have time to deliberate over my new fondness for Victoria. The forest was ablaze, and while we had somehow managed to take control of the situation, there were still fire fae refusing to back down. In my periphery, I noticed a flash of movement and turned to see the four left huddle together, plotting something that was bound to dig us into a deeper hole. I jogged to Victoria, readying an arrow. Pointing up, I asked, "Think you can bring one of those vines down?"

She nodded. "What are you thinking?"

"A little fire fae catapult."

Smiling, Victoria dropped a knee and dug her fingernails into the ground. Almost immediately, one thick vine fell from the tree top and slithered toward us. If I wasn't so impressed, I'd be super creeped out. Snakes gave me the heebie-jeebies, and vine-snakes were no different. I gagged in my mouth and reached to pick up the end of it, looping it around my arrow. "Sorry, dude," I said as I pierced the vine to secure it in place. Taking aim, I steadied my breathing and shot the arrow as far as it would go with the added weight. Thank the Faerie gods for the magic Waverly imbued in my bow because back home, the thing would have splintered instantly.

I watched the arrow fly and my lips curled upward. As it shot through the forest, the vine tightened and snapped, building in pressure from the momentum. The arrow hit something hard in the distance at the same time as the vine collided with the four fae. Their pathetic group meeting left them oblivious to any incoming attack, and a laugh escaped me as their bodies blasted backward from the hit. I counted three that hit the massive tree trunks behind them and collapsed into a heap on the ground. The other flew farther, and I watched her wrestle with the vine until she managed to free herself from it and free-fall down into the forest. She disappeared from my sight. I waited a few minutes, breathing slowly.

"I don't think she'll be back," Victoria said beside me.

"Is that the last of them?" I asked.

The witch looked around. "Looks like it. You guys showed up in the nick of time."

"You're lucky Logan figured out what the fire fae were up to," I said. "Victoria, this magic, it's—"

She held her hand up to stop me. "Dangerous," she said. "I know. But also useful if handled properly. I knew as soon as Solen started teaching me that it would put me at risk."

"So why do it?"

Victoria's eyes settled on the village. Logan had managed to put out most of the fires, but the damage was irreparable.

My heart ached for the fae that had their homes destroyed all because a few idiots tried to steal magic they had no right to. "I can use it to help them," the witch said. "Have you thought about what would happen if Billie can't stop the bomb on Earth?"

I shook my head.

"They'd all be gone, Savannah. Every last one of them. And Cathan..." She closed her eyes. "Well, who knows what he would do and if he could even free himself without Billie. But whatever it is, this realm would need help. And Logan—"

"Logan would have to stay here to keep the magic alive. To keep all five elements in balance."

She opened her eyes and looked at me. "That's why I did it even when I knew there would be fae that would want to get their hands on it, on me. Those that would want to use me to make themselves stronger. Because we all have to sacrifice something to keep Faerie alive."

When she looked away, I saw her find Solen in the mess before us, and her shoulders relaxed. Victoria definitely had something to fight for, and it sure as hell wasn't Faerie. It was who Faerie had in its grasp that made her so quick to sacrifice everything she had. My eyes focused on Logan, and my heart sank. Was I willing to sacrifice the rest of my life for him?

I thought so.

My body shivered and goosebumps formed on my arms and legs. The thought of never returning to Shadowhurst—returning home—rocked me in a way I did not expect. I cared for Logan, loved him even, but was that enough? Was that love going to satisfy me for the rest of my life? Was

Faerie? We've been in Faerie together for almost a year, but a year is very different than forever.

Feet feeling like they were covered in cement, I watched Victoria leave my side to help Logan and Solen.

Somehow, I wasn't so sure of what I wanted anymore.

Chapter Twenty

Billie

*C*athan was a lucky son of a witch, and as he sat on the floor of the library with his legs crossed and his hands magically held in place by spelled shackles, all I wanted was to wipe the smile off his smug face. If River didn't hold me back, I would have probably killed him already.

I moved in closer and noticed River's body tense beside me. "It's okay," I said. "We're good."

We were most definitely not good. We released Cathan from the jar almost a full hour ago and he had not said one word. All the bastard did was sit on the floor and smile. Every once in a while, he tugged at the shackles Sebyl placed on him and his smile widened until he resembled one of those creepy killer dolls you see in bad horror movies. I watched him carefully, eyes rolling up and down his body. He seemed smaller somehow and not quite the wretched man I remembered fighting in the cemetery. His black hair was longer now, hanging past his ears in perfect ringlets. As he tucked a strand behind one, my eyes caught on the pointy end of his left ear—the only thing that separated him from a truly human form. Cathan's sapphire eyes, my eyes, scanned the library slowly, the muscles of his square jaw twitching. The injuries he endured during our last battle had healed, and his face looked more angular and cut, as though he might have lost some weight during his time in the jar. One thing stayed the same though, and it made me gag in my mouth— Cathan continued to act like he was the best thing this world had ever seen.

His blue eyes darted to me. I held his gaze, refusing to show any sign of weakness.

"It's in your best interest to talk," I said, voice almost not trembling. "I'm getting impatient. If you have nothing to say, you're going back in there." I pointed at the jar.

I thought I saw a glimmer of disgust cross his face, at least until Luna said, "Ask him about the bomb."

At the mention of the bomb, Cathan's gross grin spread and his upper lip curled, revealing a row of shiny white teeth. He brought a hand up to his chin and scratched his beard before settling in to make himself more comfortable on the wood floor.

We messed up.

I knew in that moment that he would keep his mouth shut no matter how much we threatened him. We played into his hand. Any leverage we might have had was gone. My plan was to bluff and lie, make him think his bomb didn't work and that all we wanted to do was to figure out how to open the portal so we could get our friends out of Faerie. Then tease information out of him and hope he slips up about the bomb and how to disable it.

That plan was out the window now.

I walked to one of the bookshelves lining the walls of the

library and snatched an amber crystal. My fingers laced over the stone, its energy coursing through me as I connected to that element of my magic. My eyes flared, and I turned back to face Cathan, a fireball hovering in the air above my open palm. His one eyebrow raised, challenging me.

"Billie, what are you doing?" Beatrix asked, a worried tremor coating her words.

"Giving him some incentive," I answered.

Then I chucked the fireball at Cathan's chest.

He tried to duck out of the way, but the position in which he sat and the weight of the shackles made him slower, lazier. The fireball slammed into his chest, and I watched his eyes bulge in pain as the fire ate through his tunic and burned his flesh. Cathan let out a low hiss, one hand swatting to put out the flames. *Bet you wish you could use your magic, huh? Asswipe.*

"Babe," River warned through our bond.

I turned to him. "It's fine. I'm not trying to kill him," I said out loud. "But he'll be begging me to by the time I'm done."

With that, I formed another fireball and threw it right at Cathan's nasty face.

Two hours and twenty-eight minutes. That was how long it took for me to get tired of magically kicking Cathan's ass. It was also how long it took for him to start looking like my hits actually had an effect on him. His hair, no longer coiffed to perfection, was a disheveled matted mess atop his head and bruises spread over his skin where my magic landed harder punches.

Yet he was not talking.

At least not about anything useful.

"You know," Cathan said, his breathing labored. "I imagined more of the High Coven library. You made it seem larger than life, darling."

My mother picked up a book and flung it in his direction, but Cathan managed to shift in time. The book hit a nearby shelf, then plummeted to the floor. "I'm not your darling," she hissed out. "Haven't been in some time."

"Oh, but you will forever be mine in here." Cathan tapped his chest and pouted, laughing.

This time, the book hit him square in the jaw. I had to give it to Beatrix, she never missed twice. I stood between them, hoping to stop the bickering since it was getting us nowhere fast. While Cathan looked worse for wear, he wasn't in bad enough shape to spill his guts, and I wasn't sure I wanted to continue to waste my energy on torturing him. Especially since he seemed to enjoy the torture.

Freak.

As I stared at the half-broken man on the ground, an idea formed. He may be impervious to physical torture, but what if we tried something else? Threats were best made when they held more meaning. I pulled my phone out of my pocket and held my finger up, pretending to take a call.

"Hey, Peyton," I said to no one at all. "Aha, aha..." Turning my back, I pretended to lower my voice to keep Cathan from hearing me. "You've got to be kidding me. You didn't! How?"

From the corner of my eye, I saw Cathan's interest pique and his shoulders straightened as he leaned in to hear more of the fake conversation. I tried not to grin and continued the act. "I can't believe Victoria figured it out. How long can she keep it open for?" I stopped talking and pretended to listen. Then whispered, "We'll be there soon."

Everyone in the room stared at me with mouths agape. Everyone, including Cathan. I shoved the phone in the back pocket of my jeans and kept my back to him. Winking in a way that only River could see, I said, "We need to get to the cemetery. Now."

Turning to Cathan, I put my game face on and rolled my shoulders. "Looks like you'll have to tell us how to stop this bomb, whether you want to or not," I said sternly. "Unless you want the fae to get caught up in your plans, too."

"They wouldn't dare leave Faerie," Cathan said.

The slightest notes of fear shook his voice, and it took everything I had to keep a straight face when I said, "Logan is crossing them over as we speak. Looks like your plan had one major flaw—didn't count on the fae hating you enough to help us, did you?"

A few low gasps sounded from behind me, and I cringed. I was glad Cathan took the bait, but the thought of lying to my mom and the priestesses did not sit right with me. Yet there was no time to let them in on my plan, and they'd thank me once I got the answers we needed.

Cathan rubbed his chin again, considering what I revealed. His lips tightened into a line until they almost disappeared from his face, making him look even more sinister than he was. His eyes lowered to the floor, then were on me again, burning into the deepest core of my being. He leaned in and I tasted victory in the air. My tongue felt too big for my mouth. I snapped my teeth shut as I came closer to Cathan. The smell of Faerie and hate rolled off him in waves, so much so I had to breathe through my mouth to keep from gagging. I took a few more steps in and crouched before him. "Better start talking. You're running out of time, too."

The cowardly King of Faerie looked over my shoulder at the others and brought his lips by my ear. I sucked in a breath, ready.

"Best get moving then, dear daughter," Cathan whispered.

I bit my lips, trying to understand what he meant. What I should have done was get the hell away from him because before I knew it, Cathan's shackles were on the ground and he had his palms on either side of my head. He pulled me back, then slammed my forehead into his knee so hard, my vision swimming.

My head swam and my eyes refused to focus. A deafening whistle sounded in my ears and I swayed from side to side when I tried to stand. Muffled screams echoed through the library and I thought I heard River yell, "Get him!"

There was a scuffle near to me, somewhere by the staircase leading out of the basement. I heard a heavy thud and as I tried to focus my spotty vision, I saw my mom climb to her knees at the foot of the stairs.

Bent in half, I turned toward the spiral staircase and pressed my hands to my ears to stop the ringing. Horror crawled its way up my body as I watched Cathan run up the steps, all the way out of the library.

Chapter
Twenty-one

River

When Cathan attacked Billie, I saw red. Fur sprouted from my arms and my lip tore as my teeth sharpened and grew. I took a few quick breaths, calming the wolf and coaxing him back into his hiding spot. The last thing we needed was for my shifter form to run amuck in the High Coven's townhouse. Truce or not, there were way too many witches in this place that wouldn't think twice about vanquishing me.

Some even in this room.

"Get him!" I shouted and ran to Billie. As carefully as I could, I slid behind her and scooped my arms under hers to hold her up. She continued to sway, her eyes looking glassy and lost. The fucker knocked her out pretty bad, and this was a concussion if I'd ever seen one. "I'm going to get us closer to the wall, okay?" I asked, as I started to shimmy myself backward.

Billie nodded and her head rolled back onto my shoulder. As carefully as I could, I scooted us to the one wall free of shelves and maneuvered myself around so that Billie's back pressed to it. "Babe, I need to go after him."

"I know," she said, her words slurring. "Don't kill him."

"No promises."

I hopped up, giving her one last glance before running to the staircase. Taking two steps at a time, I ran to the upper level of the townhouse and down the main hallway. Cathan knew his way around this place from his time spent with Beatrix, but even if he didn't, it wasn't hard to make it from the library to the front door. It was literally straight ahead.

Except straight ahead was completely empty.

No door ajar, no signs of a struggle. Nothing to indicate that Cathan's escape led him in this direction.

I scratched my head and swung around, my body facing the intricate maze of the townhouse. The main hallway continued to run straight toward the back of the house, but a few smaller hallways spread out to the right and left. This place was so much bigger than it looked on the outside, and I had to wonder if magic might have had something to do with that. I made a mental note to ask Billie and stalked ahead. On either side of me, the hallways revealed closed doors with runes carved into the wooden frames holding them. Bedrooms. The smell of patchouli and rosemary penetrated my nostrils, and my eyes watered from the stench. I knew the witches used herbs in their spellwork, but did they really need so much of them?

Breathing through my mouth, I walked down the hallway until I reached the back wall. To my left, more bedrooms appeared, but to my right, only one door greeted me, the one leading to the backyard. And it was wide open.

I picked up the pace, and all but threw myself through it, tumbling out like a wild animal freed from a cage. At the far end of the yard, the high priestesses stood in a semi-circle with Beatrix in the center. In the midst of their scary-ass huddle was Cathan, though the bastard didn't appear to be afraid.

"There's nowhere for you to run," I heard Beatrix say. "Surrender, and I promise to ask them to take it easy on you."

The "them" I assumed she meant were the high priest-esses, whose hands each held a bundle of crystals, elements ready to destroy the prick that thought he could escape. Sebyl's sharp bob cut didn't even move when she summoned the wind and threw it at Cathan. Between their bodies, I watched him slide across the grass, back slamming into the wrought-iron fence encasing the yard. Next was Rhiamon, who pocketed her crystals and reached for the sword strapped to her back instead. The warrior priestess was at Cathan's side in a flash, the sharp blade of her sword pressing into his jugular. Luna and Theodora joined her, each balancing a fireball in their palms.

The blue-haired priestess came face-to-face with Cathan, snarling. "Oh, I don't know about that," she said. "Leniency is not our style."

I felt completely helpless without my wolf. Sure, I was pretty damn good in a brawl, but as much as I wanted to help, my measly fighting skills were no match for the magic the priestesses possessed. And while I didn't know Billie's mom all that well yet, I knew she was as powerful as the rest of them. More so, maybe.

Staying put, I fought the urge to grab Cathan by the throat and throttle him. For a brief moment, the fae king looked as though he might surrender. Then his eyes flicked to something past my shoulder. I froze.

"Ah, daughter dearest," Cathan said.

I spun around and watched as Billie stepped through the open doorway. Her skin had regained some color, but she was still unsteady on her feet, using the doorframe for balance. I started for her, stopping when she waved me off. Even without our bond, I knew why she refused my help despite clearly needing it. She couldn't let Cathan see he had an effect on her. Black circles lined her tired eyes and there was a large angry bump on her forehead where it met Cathan's knee. Bastard.

She held her phone up. "Tell us how to stop the bomb, and I'll tell Logan to stay put."

Keeping up the charade, I see.

I was proud of Billie for thinking quickly on her feet. The witches may not have known that she was bluffing, but I knew for a fact that no one managed to open the portal. There was no call from Peyton, and the whole thing was a ploy to get Cathan to talk. It was a good one, and it clearly worked, seeing as how we now had an escapee on our hands. One my wolf wanted to turn into a chew toy.

Billie took another hesitant step into the yard, and the high priestesses backed off Cathan to give her space. Well, all of them except Theodora, who didn't move an inch. In fact, the fireball she held only grew larger, and she continued to stare Cathan down with poison in her eyes. I always thought she was the more amicable of the four priestesses, leaving it to Sebyl to play the wicked witch, but not today. Today, Theodora was out for blood and I respected it. It seemed we had that in common when it came to Cathan.

Continuing to walk forward carefully, Billie said, "Never thought you'd be at a loss for words."

"Not a loss," Cathan replied. "Though there are no words I could give that would comfort you."

Wait, he can't mean...

My girl must have caught on the sentiment at the same time as I did because I saw the slightest droop of her shoulders as she neared Cathan. "Are you saying we can't stop the bomb?"

The fae licked his lips. "I'm saying *you* can't, daughter of mine."

"Who, then? You?"

"Oh, no. Most definitely not me," Cathan said. "To stop that which is inevitable would take a power neither of us possesses. Only the selfless can help the selfish."

Billie marched right up to him, raised her hand, and slapped him across the face. Actually slapped him. Needles pricked my skin, and the excitement I felt in that moment was more than obvious. Finally! No more chit-chat, no more playing this idiot's game. *Kick his ass, babe!*

"No!" Billie said, raising her hand again. "I'm sick of your riddles. Speak clearly or I swear I will step aside and watch as they tear you apart."

The threat landed because Cathan's cocky grin dissipated and was replaced by a darkness I well remembered of the fae king. It was the same look he had when he tortured me in Faerie. Inside, the wolf whined and my leg muscles tensed in my jeans. A warning of danger.

I looked around the yard. What were we not seeing that Cathan was?

While my body was turned away, a bright flash blurred in my periphery. Something hard hit my back and sent me flying across the backyard. My shoulder blades ached, and heat spread from them all the way down my body. I glanced over my shoulder, panic setting in.

I was on fire.

Rolling from front to back, I squirmed on the ground like a complete tool until I could no longer feel the burn spreading over my body. My back throbbed and steam rose from me, but I managed to put it all out. Lying on the ground, I looked at Billie and the witches, terror settling over me.

Theodora, her blue hair wild and her kohl-lined eyes narrowed, blasted the others with fireballs bigger than a medium-sized dog. Behind her, Cathan gripped the top of the iron fence and proceeded to hoist himself over. His foot pushed off the railing and he landed on the opposite side of the yard in a crouch.

All the while Theodora continued to attack her own people.

Around her, darkness billowed. I looked from her to Cathan, watching as he twirled his fingers, matching her every move. The bastard had gotten a grip on her somehow and was commanding her body like a damn puppeteer. His hands fluidly sliced the air and Theodora launched a ball of fire, barely missing Sebyl's head. The high priestess growled and put her hands up, firing a gust of wind at Theodora. As the yard spun into a tangle of fire, water, wind, and blue hair, I turned my attention on Cathan.

He watched the fiasco through the bars, one hand commanding Theodora while the other raised over his head. That couldn't be good. I jumped up, crossing the yard in seconds. As Cathan lowered his arm, I climbed over the fence. When black shadows swirled around his body, I dropped on the other side. And when the shadows cleared, revealing an emptiness where Cathan once stood, I fisted my hands and let out a loud scream. We fucking lost him.

Chapter
Twenty-two

Logan

I sat with my back against a charred tree while Savannah and Victoria faffed around, attempting to clear the rubble. There was no bloody way we'd ever restore this village. At least not anytime soon. Looking past the trees and into the thickness of the forest, I thumped my head against the trunk and sighed. Why was everything so damn difficult all the time?

Above me, the sky turned to a deeper shade of purple, Faerie's version of evening rolling around. I sucked in cool air through my teeth and sighed.

"We can move everyone south tomorrow," a familiar voice said.

I cleared my throat and turned my head to get a clearer view of Waverly. Her shoulders were more hunched than usual, and I briefly wondered if my pathetic version of kingship finally broke the loyal fae. "When did you make it down here?"

"Right around the time you started daydreaming," she said. "Care to share what has you so distracted?"

While the fae's words carried no insult, I felt like a proper git. Everyone was busy trying to fix the village—to no avail—and here I was, sitting on the job. As much as I tried to ignore it, there was a sinking feeling deep in my gut telling me I wasn't faring much better than Cathan in the king department.

Towering over me, Waverly rolled her neck.

"I'm worried," I admitted.

"About the village?"

My leg muscles tensed and the fabric of my trousers stretched over them, suddenly too hot to bear. Eyes narrowing to slits, I slumped against the massive tree trunk. "The village, Cathan, this entire realm," I said. "All of it, really."

For a long while, Waverly stayed silent. I started to wonder if I said anything at all or if I was simply imaging the entire bloody conversation. I knocked my head a couple times during the gruesome altercation at the village and there was a pretty good chance I was hallucinating. Or worse. *Blimey. Am I dead?*

Gaze traveling across the rubble, I spotted Savannah and my stomach tensed. She yelled commands right and left, ordering the fae around like she ran the place. I couldn't help but laugh. Even in my afterlife, Savannah was a force to be reckoned with.

"This is amusing to you?"

My eyes widened. I ran a hand through my hair, a knot catching in my fingers. Peeling my eyes from Savannah, I looked at the narrow-eyed fae standing with her arms crossed before me. *Not dead then. Brilliant.* I forced a meek smile and retied my matted hair. Perhaps if I closed my eyes, Waverly would go away and let me have a moment of peace.

I felt like a right tosser thinking about it, and yet I couldn't help but blink for a little longer than usual. The fae tapped her foot on the ground impatiently.

So much for getting a break.

"Sorry," I finally muttered. "This is likely not what you expected of your new king."

To my utter surprise, Waverly laughed. Her voice rose several octaves, and she continued to laugh so loud, it attracted the attention of a few people in the distance. They stopped what they were doing and stared in our direction until Savannah caught them slacking and scolded them back to their tasks. After a few more tear-filled chuckles, Waverly finally simmered down. "I'm not sure if you recall," she said, wiping her eyes, "but our last king was not exactly favorable. Considering that you are yet to treat our kind as prisoners, you can laugh at our adversity all you like."

"Oh, I wasn't—"

She shook me off with the brush of a hand. "It matters little. I could not imagine what you are going through considering the situation in Shadowhurst, and yet I fear I must ask you to put it aside. At least for now." Waverly gestured to Victoria, who was using her abysmally odd magic to lift a fallen tree off the ground. "Everyone seems to be working together. It would be helpful for them to see their king at their side."

Once more, I wanted to shut the fae away. Could she not see I was doing the best I could under the circumstances? I was bloody here, wasn't I? In their realm, trying to keep the entire thing from going bollocks up, when I could have easily left and let Billie stay behind as she originally planned. My chest constricted, and I swallowed a massive lump in my throat. What was I on about? These weren't strangers. The fae were my kind, too, and the closest to family I had outside of Billie and Savannah. Sure, they were full of angst and sordid issues I couldn't yet understand, but what family was perfect? None that I knew. I thought back to my first few weeks at the resistance house and how astonishingly different the experience was. If I could find my place in a house full of shadowers, I could sure as hell find it here.

Besides, Waverly was right. The fae needed to see me in action.

Straining against spreading bruises, I rose to stand. My pulse thundered through my head, but I brushed it off, focusing instead on the tasks needing to be completed. "We should move everyone into the castle for the evening. There are plenty of beds and I don't think we can get the village back in order quickly enough. These people need a place to stay until we can relocate them." I looked at Waverly. "You mentioned going south? Isn't that a gamble with the fire fae taking residence there?"

"We can take alternate routes," she replied. "There are several spots the fire fae do not inhabit that offer good grounds for another village. It will take time, but I think we can manage for a short while."

"Good," I said. "That's good." I glanced around, my eyes catching on Victoria. "Can I ask you a question?"

The fae nodded for me to continue.

"What's your opinion of Victoria's magic?"

My question hung in the air for much too long to be comfortable. When Waverly answered, I could sense she was being diplomatic in her response. "It is a rare skill to learn for fae folk," she said. "For a human witch to know how to create Faerie magic is unheard of."

As much as I appreciated her not overstepping, I needed

some brutal honesty. I had gotten much too used to Savannah never holding back to want anything but. I eyed Waverly carefully, then asked, "What do you really think?"

"That Solen was a fool to get her tangled up in it."

I smiled. "Agreed. Do you think she's in danger because of it?"

Waverly cocked one eyebrow and gestured to the village. I frowned.

"If we can convince Solen and Victoria to lie low, we can protect them until things settle," the fae said. "Though I believe you have more pressing matters to consider. Even if your friends in Shadowhurst dispel the bomb without forcing our kind to leave this place, how long does Faerie have?"

I tried to understand what she meant, but drew a bloody blank. As far as I knew, Faerie was not in any danger now that Cathan was not in power, and with my choice to stay here, we had all the elements in place to guarantee its survival. What did Waverly mean? Was there more I should be worried about? My head hurt thinking about adding issues to the pile of dung I was already in.

Sucking in a deep breath, I faced her head on. "Is there something I wasn't told when I took over Cathan's position as king?"

"Not at all," Waverly answered. Her eyes turned to slits, and she steeled her spine, standing nearly as tall as me now. "I would have thought it was obvious. Cathan was fae. You are not."

"And?" I shrugged.

"Our time in Faerie and its existence is linked to the life-line of the fae residing here. It is linked to their elemental magic. Cathan's magic, all our magic, is eternal. Yours…"

Her words slapped me in the face. How could I have been so bloody stupid? Half fae or not, I was not going to live forever. Even with time in Faerie moving slower, there would come a time when my life would end and what would happen to the realm then? Unless Savannah and I had children—my heart spasmed thinking about it—this place was doomed. And if we did, then what? Was I truly willing to force my kids to stay here simply to keep the realm going? I wasn't sure.

There was always Billie, but I doubted she'd consider it. Her life was in Shadowhurst, her children's lives would be as well.

To sum up, we were properly screwed.

Shoulders tenser than they had been in weeks, I rubbed the back of my neck and looked out over the remnants of the village. Fae of all elements crowded the destroyed space, helping each other where they could. Despite the events of the day, their faces betrayed no emotions. They simply did what was needed to get the job done. Amongst them, Savannah and Victoria followed suit. Shaking my numb legs off, I strode away from Waverly to join the others. Sadness loomed in the depths of my chest, but I brushed it off.

No matter what awaited us in the future—near or distant—I was here now. There was no dwelling on matters in Faerie. My only hope was that if it came time to leave this realm, the fae would do exactly what they were doing right now. That they would do whatever was necessary to survive.

Somehow, I doubted it would be that bloody easy.

Chapter
Twenty-three

Billie

"This way!"

I skidded to a stop on the hard pavement and made a sharp right turn. At the end of the street, my mother stood with her arm outstretched and her index finger pointing down a narrow alley. I wasn't sure how she guessed Cathan's trajectory, but we'd been doing a decent enough job of keeping up with the slippery fool. So far, we tracked him across the city and into the less favorable part of town. The air stank of sewage and week-old garbage, and I tried not to vomit as I rounded the corner and nipped into the alley after Beatrix. My head was a hot mess from the townhouse incident, and I was pretty sure I had a mild concussion. The foul stench of the alley was definitely not helping.

Footsteps pounded the ground behind me, and River yelled for me to slow down. No way. I wasn't letting Cathan get away, and judging from the speed with which Beatrix bulleted down the dark passage, neither was she.

My breath hitched as I picked up the pace to keep up with her. "Are you sure he went this way?"

"Yes!" she replied, not bothering to turn around. "I know all his hiding spots in the city."

The nausea was back in full force, now that an image of my mom and Cathan sneaking off for their gross little rendezvous crowded my mind. For as long as I lived, I would never understand how Beatrix fell for his crap. In her defense, I almost did as well when we met the bastard in Faerie, but Beatrix really took the cake. The woman had a child with the monster.

"Through here!"

Snapping myself out of my head, I followed her past a stack of decrepit old crates to what appeared to be a dead end. A large brick wall rose before us, and my feet worked overtime to make sure I didn't collide with the damn thing face first. I looked around the tight space, confused. "There's nothing here."

"You sure about that?" Beatrix asked. Her widening grin told me I shouldn't judge a book by its cover. I was about to ask her for an explanation when my mom skirted around the crates and vanished.

"Mom?" I asked. "What the hell?"

"Where did she go?" River asked, slowing to stand beside me. On his heels, the high priestesses and Catarina caught up with us, their eyes darting around the alley. "Am I missing something here?"

I shrugged. "I think we all are."

Giving his hand a squeeze, I followed Mom's footsteps and peeked around the crates. It was so dark in the crevice between them and the brick wall, I couldn't make out an inch before me. Swallowing the excess spit my mouth decided to produce for no good reason, I stretched out my hand and felt the wall. Except there was nothing there.

Where one would expect brick, only emptiness existed. My hand fell through the void. I stumbled, my shoulder colliding with one crate. Searing pain ripped down my side and I winced, straightening myself out. Careful not to smash into anything again, I squeezed behind the crates and into the dark opening.

"Holy crap..."

"Neat, right?"

I jumped at the sound of Beatrix's voice in front of me. Or what I assumed was in front of me because I couldn't see a damn thing. My arms shot out. I felt around, fingers grazing her shoulders. "What is this place?"

"One of our old haunts," Beatrix said, as though that explained anything. "Follow me. It's not too far now."

"Not too far to get where, exactly?"

Beatrix didn't answer, and I felt the air whoosh as she departed. With a huff, I followed her into the nothingness spreading wide before us, praying to the Goddess that River and the others were close behind.

Not only was this strange, creepy passageway dark, it was also quiet as sin. I could hear every breath escaping from my overworked lungs, and the sound of my heart beating reminded me of a hammer pounding a nail. I swallowed, cringing as my slurping echoed down the passageway. I was about to ask Mom to stop when a light split my vision. My eyes spotted, and I half-shut them, following the blinding bright light in the near distance. Hot fingers gripped my arm and pulled me forward. My feet stumbled as I fell into the glow, a scream hanging on the edge of my lips.

Slowly, my sight adjusted and my jaw unhinged. The secret passageway Beatrix led us down led into a massive greenhouse. All around me, bright green leaves and colorful florals grew in a wild mess of immense beauty. The air was fresh and wet, and the mist from an overhead sprinkler system made my hair frizz up.

I stifled a gasp and found my mother a few steps ahead. "This is so—"

"Gorgeous, right?" she asked, nodding.

"What is this place?"

Beatrix smiled, her eyes far away and full of memories. "Someplace that used to hold fond memories for me."

I wanted to reach out and hug her, but thought better of it. Despite us having mended our relationship, or at least as best as we could for now, Mom and I were never a hugging family. A fist bump, maybe. But not hugs. Still, it seemed if there was ever a time to try something new, this was it. I shuffled my feet, inching closer.

I didn't make it a foot when a flash of light pierced the air and something hot struck my shoulder. My body spun around from the force, and I screamed as a burning sensation spread down my arm. Legs buckling under my imbalanced weight, I tried to right myself but didn't make it. My side hit the hard ground. I yelled out, the heat on my arm intensifying.

"Billie! Get your jacket off!"

River's voice dragged me from my thoughts and my eyes flashed to my arm. And the freaking fire spreading over it. Everything in me fought the urge to scream as I shook myself out of the burning leather. The jacket fell to the ground in a flaming heap, and I stomped on it with my boot until it was nothing but smoke and embers. My teeth ground together. *Damn it! That was my favorite jacket!*

Anger boiled to the surface as I tore my attention away from the sad pile on the floor and fixed it on the greenhouse.

More fireballs flew through the air, one zooming by and missing me by mere inches. I followed its trajectory, a steely gaze falling on the fridge-shaped fire fae standing between two large ferns. Not wasting a minute, I kicked up my boot and removed my dagger from its compartment, flicking it in the fae's direction. The blade sliced through the air, impaling itself into the beast's huge arm.

The bastard howled.

His back collided with a shelf of potted roses and the entire thing clattered to the ground. While the fae worked on removing my dagger from his arm, I scanned the area. The others had emerged through the opening of the passageway and were holding their own against six larger-than-life fire fae that seemed to have appeared out of nowhere. One after the other, the fae blasted us with magic, and yet something wasn't sitting right with me. The attack was a surprise, one that should have been much more catastrophic. But no one—except my lucky jacket—was hurt. It was like the fae weren't even trying. Either Beatrix caught them off guard or—

My blood ran cold.

"It's a trap!" I yelled out.

I was too late.

Before the words even left my lips, a spot of black appeared in my periphery. My neck twisted to see its source, and my jaw tightened when I spotted Cathan standing at the farthest side of the greenhouse. There was a doorway right behind him, and his body was half in and half out, almost like he was about to flee. Arm outstretched, Cathan's eyes met mine, and a slimy grin spread across his even slimier face. I glanced at his fingers, horror crawling down my body.

Hanging off his index and thumb were the familiar remnants of shadow magic.

I started to move for him, but a blood-curdling scream stopped me in my tracks. Against my better judgment, I forced myself away from Cathan and turned around. The fire fae were nowhere to be seen and our entire party gathered in a circle ten feet from me. Briskly, I jogged toward them, pushing my way by River and Catarina. My heart sank as I saw my mother on the ground, a pool of blood forming under her left thigh.

"Mom!" I screamed, landing beside her. Hot tears stung my lids, and I blinked them away, trying to see how badly she was hurt. "What happened? Are you okay?"

Beatrix shook her head, her chin nodding to her right.

Bile coated my mouth as I looked to where she pointed. Next to my mother, Sebyl, Rhiamon, and Luna sat on the dirty ground. Their shoulders were hunched and their hands clasped together to form a circle. Quiet whispers rose in the air around them, and I didn't have to listen to know what they were doing. The high priestesses were performing a passing ritual for a sister witch fallen in battle.

The knot in my throat grew, and I choked on it, my eyes never leaving the stiff body lying in the center of the circle.

On the ground of the greenhouse lay Theodora. Her blue hair spread loose around her like a pool of water. Her eyes were shut and her lips were slightly parted, like she was about to speak. Tears streamed down my face as I ran my gaze down her body.

All the way to her chest and the dark, black hole that formed in the place her heart should be.

Chapter
Twenty-four

Billie

*T*his is not happening. This is not happening. This is not happening.

My thoughts ran a mile a minute as I tried to process the scene in the greenhouse. The disgusting iron smell of blood in the air made me gag. I pressed my palm to my mouth, trying to keep down my breakfast. Body fighting the need to move, I stayed glued to one spot, my eyes on the high priestesses. On my arms, the mate marks wriggled over my skin and I could feel heat emanating from them as River's emotions hit me head on.

"We will tear the flesh off his bones!"

Sebyl's voice echoed through the greenhouse; I swore even the plants recoiled from the venom in them. *This is not happening.*

"*Breathe, babe,*" River instructed through our bond.

I sucked in air, only now realizing I was holding my breath. How long was I doing that for? I didn't know, but my head was dizzy, and I wanted to vomit all over my boots, so it must have been a while. Daring to glance at my mother, relief washed over me when I saw her stand up on her bad leg. The blood loss stopped, thanks to a scarf Catarina wrapped tightly around her thigh, and she wasn't as wobbly as I would have imagined. Whatever wound she had must have been superficial. Unlike...

Bile filled my mouth and the tears I tried not to shed before fell down my face like a dam broke open. My history with the high priestesses was not exactly rainbows and puppies, but losing one of them—especially Theodora—hit me in a way I didn't expect. I briefly wondered if I would feel the same ache in my chest if it were Sebyl lying lifeless on the floor instead. I wasn't sure. What I was absolutely damn sure of was, sordid history or not, a witch was dead and it was all my fault. Even though it wasn't my idea I was the one who convinced everyone to free Cathan. I was the one who pushed and pushed and pushed until I got my way. Sebyl always told me my stubborn streak was going to get me in trouble one day—why didn't I listen to her? Why didn't I let the high priestesses talk me out of my idiotic plans?

Because I put Faerie and my pathetic need to rid the world of Cathan first. And now Theodora was dead because of it.

My eyes drifted to the dark hole in her unmoving chest.

This isn't happening.

"Babe, I know you're not in a good place, but you need to see this."

River's warning dragged me out of the self-pity parade I led, and back to the greenhouse. My jaw tensed and my stomach lurched when I saw Sebyl storm away from the others and toward the back door through which Cathan and his lackeys escaped. Shit!

Careful to steer clear of Theodora and the other two

priestesses who remained by her side, I skirted around the group and headed after Sebyl. As I passed, I caught my mother's eyes, and she nodded before returning her attention to the circle cast around the body. I noticed her fingers entwined with Luna and Rhiamon, and gritted my teeth. Despite this being a traumatic event for us all, I did not like her being this close to the high priestesses. Something about it rubbed me the wrong way.

My legs picked up speed as I struggled to keep up with Sebyl's retreating back. For a woman her age, she sure moved fast. The fury driving her probably had a lot to do with it. I squeezed through the opening of the back door and yelled out, "Sebyl! Wait!"

To my surprise, the high priestess slowed her stride. Her sharp bob swayed as she spun around to face me, and I was taken aback by the sheer anger on her face. I had never seen Sebyl lose her decorum, and it was shocking to watch her show any emotion at all. Especially not this obviously.

"Where are you going?" I asked.

"He must pay," was all the high priestess said.

"Sebyl, please," I begged. "You can't go after him. Not yet. We need to recoup, talk it out, make a plan. Whether we like it or not, Cathan is our only chance of saving all magical creatures. You can't—"

Sebyl's hand shot up, silencing me. "Enough!" she roared. "You no longer decide what the High Coven will or will not do. You are a traitor, a shadower supporter, and I have let this go on long enough. Theodora is dead! Our high priestess is gone, and the coven has grown soft under your misguided influence. We will destroy the fallen fae king like we destroyed his kind before. The fae answer to us! He answers to us!"

Shaking, Sebyl started to leave, and I ran around to stand in her way.

"Step aside, child," the high priestess hissed. "Or you will not have a leg left to stand on."

For the first time since I left the High Coven, I was actually afraid of Sebyl. Not that I didn't think she could have squashed me like a bug before today, but something about her current state of mind put the fear of the Goddess in me. The high priestess was out for blood and nothing, no one, was getting in her way. Especially not the girl responsible for her sister's death. I swallowed the lump in my throat and spread my legs wider apart.

Staying true to her word, Sebyl raised her hands up, and I saw the familiar red sparkle of an amber crystal between her fingers. The witch was going to burn me where I stood if I didn't budge.

Stupidly, I stayed still.

Sebyl tsked and shook her head, then threw her hands out toward me. As she thrust, her magic jumped to the surface of her skin and a blazing line trailed between us. The fire shot forward, picking up speed and racing straight for my chest. The woman was not messing around. I spun on my heels, dodging the fatal blow with seconds to spare. As I rebounded, I felt the heat of another attack at my back. Ducking down, I hit the ground chest first and flattened myself out, the flames zooming by above me.

Determined steps sounded behind me and I readied for Sebyl to blast me right in the back. On my chest, the mate marks spread, and I felt River's worry through our bond. I had been gone much too long now. I started to call for him and stopped when a strong gust of wind swarmed the alley I lay in. The sound of something sliding across the ground filled my ears, followed by a loud thud. I pressed my palms into the rough pavement, pushing up high enough to roll over.

My body tensed and I froze.

In the open doorway stood Beatrix, her hair flying wildly around her as the wind she summoned picked up momentum. Her palms faced outward and her eyes were wider than the moon. Across the alley, Sebyl was splayed against a brick wall, the wind holding her in place. Beatrix cast me a quick glance, then reached further out. Wind flew from her fingertips and slashed across Sebyl's face. The high priestess hissed and struggled to get free, but my mom held her own.

"No more nonsense," mom said. "We don't fight each other, not now."

"You do not speak for the High Coven!" Sebyl screeched.

Not missing a beat, Beatrix grinned. "Neither do you. Without the fourth high priestess, your position in the coven is compromised. Until Theodora is replaced, any and all decisions regarding magic use must be made by the entire coven. Every. Single. Witch."

Holy crap. Mom was right. I completely forgot about the rule the High Coven had in place for occasions exactly like this. Four high priestesses. Four elements and the coven to bind them. It was an ancient law and one that was never changed. Whatever Sebyl was planning to do to Cathan, she couldn't do it without the entire coven casting a vote. *Loophole!*

I smiled, then quickly straightened my lips out. Rubbing my overwhelming joy in Sebyl's face was not going to make any of this easier. In the doorway, mom's eyes met Sebyl's, and she said, "I'm going to let you go and we're going inside to take care of Theodora. All three of us."

Slowly and while keeping a watchful eye on Sebyl, she lowered her hands, and the wind died away. The high priestess's body relaxed, and she dropped down the few inches she was hovering, landing on the balls of her feet. Her eyes shot daggers at me as she rubbed her wrists before tucking her hands into the pockets of her blood-colored suit jacket. At her gesture of surrender, my mother nodded and stepped aside, leaving ample space in the doorway for both of us to pass. Silently, we walked back into the greenhouse, not making eye contact. My body grew rigid with each step and I watched as Sebyl's shoulders rose and fell with angry breaths ahead of me. At my back, Mom's steady steps followed us inside, and I took comfort in knowing she was on my side. I wasn't sure when it happened, but Beatrix had become a voice of reason for the high priestesses, even Sebyl. The stubborn witch never backed down until today, and I wondered what it was my mother did to make her so important to the High Coven. It couldn't have simply been the last few weeks of working together.

I made a mental note to ask her about it later.

As we neared the others, River jogged up to my side and squeezed my waist, pulling me into himself. I forced a meek smile and steeled my spine to get ready for what came next. With her back to me, Sebyl joined her sisters in the circle, kneeling. Her head bowed as she reached over to place two celestite crystals on each of Theodora's closed lids and I tried not to think about how perfectly they matched the color of her hair. My head lowered instinctively to match Sebyl's gesture.

"What do we do now?" River whispered in my ear.

I closed my eyes, my lungs paper-thin in my chest. As the high priestesses began their incantation, I heard my mother's trembling voice join in and sadness poured over me. One more witch down. One more friend lost. One more empty chair at the table later. How many was I willing to sacrifice to rid the world of the vermin that was my father? *None,* I told myself. I would not let anyone else get hurt, and the only way to do it was to put my big-girl pants on and do what I should have done long ago. I had to find Cathan and end him for good. The only problem was, I had no idea where he went or how to get him to spill the information we needed before I stabby-stabbed the bastard.

Shaking, I peeled my lids apart and looked at the circle. "Now we bury our friend," I said. "And then I'm going hunting."

Chapter Twenty-five

Logan

*N*ights at the palace were excruciatingly long, even more so now that the place was overrun by fae. Voices carried down the dimly lit corridor I walked down. I hurried my pace, trying to avoid another bloody session of small talk. It seemed after we managed to secure beds for the fae affected by the battle, everyone and their sodding mother needed a word with me. I did my best to smile and nod and listen to their unnecessary thank you's, but after a while, all I wanted was to find a dark corner somewhere and hide for all of eternity.

Who knew being a king meant so much chit-chat?

I doubted Cathan spent any of his time making pals with the fae he governed. Then again, it was impossible to be friendly when you're out to oppress and destroy your own subjects. Acid filled my mouth. The simple thought of the fae being my subjects made my stomach turn. Deep down, I knew I had to step up and lead these people, but I was going to avoid that for as long as possible. No matter how much Savannah bugged me over it.

A rare smile crossed my face.

I couldn't wait to get this day over with so I could spend some time with her.

"Finally!"

Stopping dead in my tracks, I snapped my jaw shut, dreams of being alone for a few moments quickly evaporating. I cracked my neck and retied my hair into a knot to buy myself time before another ambush of pointless chatter. Slower than molasses, I turned on my heel to face whatever fae needed me.

To my utter surprise, Solen's impatient glare greeted me at the end of the long hallway. "I have been up and down this maze of a palace trying to find you."

I worked my jaw, eating the choice words I had for Victoria's favorite fae.

"Come with me," Solen urged.

Crossing my arms, I cocked an eyebrow and tipped my chin. "Can this wait until the morning, mate? I was about to tuck in."

"Would I be here if it could wait?" Solen asked, already walking away. "Victoria and Savannah are in the library. We should hurry."

At the sound of Savannah's name mentioned, I picked up my stride to keep up with the fae. As we darted down the corridor, the glass walls of the palace frosted over to block out the rooms we passed, hiding the fae inside from view. Living in this bloody place was like spending all your time in a video game. It was exhausting. Solen rounded the corner and took the stairs down to the bottom level. When he reached it, I yelled out, "Why are they even there at this hour?"

Solen didn't break his stride. In fact, he sped up a little

right before yelling back, "Victoria believes she found a solution to your problem on Earth. We must hurry!"

I all but flew into the library after I heard what Solen was in a knot about. With everything that's been happening, I knew better than to get my hopes up, but something about this new revelation had me buzzing. Pushing the doors wide open, I rushed into the library and skidded to a stop. Near one of the large, arched windows facing the rear gardens, Victoria and Savannah stood facing out, their voices carrying in hushed tones across the room. I couldn't make out what they said, but whatever it was, it must have been serious. Savannah's entire body was rigid as stone and her shoulders hiked up so high they grazed the bottom of her earlobes.

Clearing my throat, I tiptoed into the room like a bloody stalker, with Solen close on my heels.

"There you are," Savannah expelled a breath, turning around to face me. "I thought we lost you for good."

I closed the distance between us and pressed my lips to her forehead, inhaling the fresh scent of her shampoo. "Don't you wish, love."

Savannah nudged her elbow in my ribs and I grunted, chuckling. Then, turning to Victoria, said, "Solen mentioned you had an idea to disable the bomb."

"Not disable, exactly," the witch said.

Blimey. I should have known it was too good to be true. I cast Solen a death glare and swallowed hard, the muscles in my stomach tightening. Getting my hopes up was a mistake. Why did I think we would have any luck, when Billie and the entire High Coven failed to come up with a plan? Not only were our resources slim to none—considering we were in another bloody realm that didn't even have an internet connection—but our collective experience with this was disturbingly limited. All we had to depend on were the fae at our disposal and Victoria's witch magic. We hadn't even been able to locate the final piece of the puzzle Cathan left behind, despite having turned the entire realm over looking for it. To sum up, we were properly screwed.

"I think I can stop the bomb from destroying everyone on Earth," Victoria added.

My ears burnt. "What? How?"

The witch drifted away from the window and stood by Solen, her fingers running absently along the edge of one book on a shelf. Looking at her now in the dim evening glow of the library, I realized how much Victoria had changed since we got here. All of us had to adapt to Faerie, but Victoria didn't adapt, she reinvented herself. If it wasn't for me knowing her prior to all of this, I would have easily confused her for fae. Her sleeve rolled down and for a second, I thought I saw the markings of a tattoo on her forearm before Victoria dropped her arm. I glanced between her and Solen. Had Savannah and I changed as much, too?

"Honestly," Victoria started, "I'm surprised I didn't think of it sooner."

My anticipation leapt to new heights, and a rumble resembling a low growl vibrated in my chest. "Quit faffing around and get to it, please. You lot are killing me here."

Next to me, Savannah grimaced. I looked between the three of them, trying to decipher what I was missing. Whatever Victoria figured out, it was starting to sound a lot less promising than before.

"There's a witch on Earth," Victoria explained. "She was one of the High Coven sisters when I was younger until she messed around with magic the high priestesses didn't approve of. Needless to say, she wasn't part of the coven after that."

I must have been a sodding fool because I was drawing a complete blank as to how this helped our situation. "What does this witch have to do with the bomb? Do you think she'll know how to diffuse it?"

"No," Victoria said harshly. "The magic Torine practiced was all about energy. Mainly, she was experimenting with transferring energy from one place to another."

Rubbing my temples, I narrowed my eyes in her direction. "That doesn't sound all that terrible."

Victoria scoffed. "It wasn't, until Torine took it upon herself to transfer energy from a sister witch. That's when the coven stepped in and kicked her to the curb."

The group let go of a collective sigh, and I looked around like a bloody buffoon. I was having trouble keeping up. Why did I care about this Torine person? She sounded like a selfish piece of work, and while what Victoria explained of her power was impressive, a witch shunned by the High Coven was the least of my concern.

Trying not to look like a tosser, I forced out a weak smile, coating my words with honey. "What happened to the witch whose energy she stole?"

"Nothing good," Victoria said. She didn't elaborate, and I guessed it was a disastrous outcome. I knew little of the details of witch magic, but I knew enough to understand that draining someone magical energy is akin to death for a witch. Torine was a sodding monster from the sounds of it.

Leaning into Savannah, I furrowed my brow. "What does our situation have to do with her?"

"I think she can help," Victoria answered. "The magic Torine practiced was not one I've heard of another witch trying since. It's dangerous and dark and very frowned upon. I doubt even the rogues want anything to do with it. But in our case, it might be our only chance."

"How?" The answer came to me before Victoria had a chance to explain. "You want her to transfer the energy from the bomb. Is that even possible?"

The witch nodded and her hand slipped into Solen's. "It should be. The bomb, wherever it is, is magic, right? And anything made with magic has an energy to it. Fae or witch or shadower, it doesn't matter. If it's magical, Torine can hone in on its source."

"This is great!" I yelled, nearly jumping for joy. "It solves everything!"

"Not quite," Savannah whispered beside me. Her eyes burrowed into me and she worried at her bottom lip, her palm squeezing my arm. "The energy from the bomb would have to go somewhere else. Somewhere it can be contained."

Here we go. Nothing could ever be simple when it came to magic, and it sure as bloody hell couldn't be simple where Cathan was concerned. Of *course* there had to be a problem. Why would I expect anything else? The headache I'd been fighting to suppress exploded behind my eyes, and I bit the inside of my cheek to keep from smashing things. "Can Billie and the witches create some sort of enclosure, the way they did to trap Cathan?"

Victoria shook her head. "It won't be strong enough. Cathan created this thing to have a massive impact; containing its energy will require more than a simple vessel. The bomb is volatile. Torine would need to transfer its energy somewhere we know can take the hit if the stupid thing was to go off."

"Where would we..." My mouth dried up. "Faerie. You

want her to transfer the bomb's energy here and wait for it to go boom, don't you?"

The witch nodded in agreement, and my entire body recoiled. There was no more time for second guessing. The fae had to leave whether they wished to or not. My head pounded when I thought about what that would mean. It was as though everything I had tried so hard to avoid came crashing down on me. I couldn't breathe. I pushed back on my heels and walked to the window, opening it wide. My eyes scanned the gardens and guilt pricked at the rear of my mind. I couldn't begin to imagine how the fae would react. Blimey. The fire fae. We were in for some serious destruction once news got out that everyone had to leave or die.

A part of me—the selfish, childish part—wished Torine would turn us down. Even though I'd never admit it, I liked Faerie. Mostly, I liked the possibility of what it could mean for Savannah and me. Now, not only did I have to convince a bunch of powerful, angry fae to leave the only home they'd ever known, but I had no time to do it. Times like this, I almost wished I was as much of a careless prick as Cathan was. I cringed, shaking the thoughts away and jostling myself back to reality.

I would never be like my father.

"We need to tell the fae," I said. "As soon as possible, so they have time to make their peace with what's coming."

"We will," Savannah agreed. "But first need to get a message to Billie."

I turned to look at her over my shoulder. "Right. She needs to get to this witch ASAP."

"Faster than you know," Victoria added. "If I thought of it, I'm sure Cathan did as well. Torine might be in danger.

Solen will warn Billie immediately; we must prepare on our end as well. Torine might require my help."

Blood cooling in my veins, I peered out the window again. "There's one more problem," I told the others. "We still don't know how to open the portal. Unless your witch can help with that, we're bloody stuck."

Chapter
Twenty-six

Billie

*B*lack dots swarmed my vision as I peeled my lids apart, waking up from a nap that was much too short. I didn't even remember falling asleep. One minute I was minding my own business on an oversized, antique ottoman at the coven's townhouse, and the next Solen was breathing down my neck. At some point, I needed to discuss dream privacy with the water fae. Though I couldn't be too mad, considering the good news the hottie delivered.

I rubbed my eyes and forced my shaking legs to stand. Not far from where I crashed, hushed voices carried through the hallway and I followed them to find my mom, Sebyl, and Catarina lounging in the main sitting room. Each woman held a saucer filled with steaming tea, and they chatted as though they were friends catching up and not three powerful witches who would be trying to kill each other if it weren't for bigger problems. At one point, I was pretty sure I saw Sebyl smile.

What is happening right now?

Throat suddenly full, I swallowed audibly and leaned in the open doorway, my arms crossed.

"Good morning," Mom said with a smirk. "Get some rest?"

I pointed between her and the two witches. "How long was I out for? Are you three friends now? What year is this?"

Mom chuckled and placed her cup down on the coffee table. "Always so dramatic. We were brainstorming the next course of action."

Of course they were. It was too much to ask for these three to get over themselves and make peace already. I would have thought after what happened to Theodora, they might have a new perspective on magic, but it wasn't looking like we would ever get there. My heart gave a jolt as I fought away the memories of burying the high priestess only hours ago. The ceremony was rushed, considering our circumstance, but it was everything Theodora would have wanted. Sebyl organized a circle casting in the High Coven's backyard, and even the rogues were allowed to show up. I was certain if we lived through what was coming for us, there would be a bigger, more intense ceremony performed, especially since the coven needed to pick a new high priestess. My gut twisted into knots.

Under a day left on the clock.

"So, about that..." I rubbed the rear of my neck. "I might have an idea of our next steps. Well, Victoria does."

"Victoria?" Sebyl's thin eyebrows dipped under her stiff bangs.

"Yep. Solen had a message for me while I was out. Victoria thinks we can transfer the energy from the bomb into Faerie, but to do it we need—"

"Torine Beaumont," Sebyl interrupted. "Absolutely not.

We will not associate with Torine. She is not welcome in this coven and she is not a witch you want to work with. Believe me when I tell you nothing good can come from involving Torine."

Sliding down in the doorway, I tried to come up with a diplomatic way to tell Sebyl to suck it. If this witch was bad news, I frankly didn't care. Sebyl and her coven minions were not exactly on my list of friends, and yet here we all were, working together. I needed Sebyl to see that she was being unreasonable. We were running out of time.

Pressing my shoulder blades into the wood frame, I fixed my eyes on the high priestess. "I don't know how to say this nicely," I said. My mother mumbled something under her breath, but it was too late to stop me now. "We have under twenty-four hours before a fae-created bomb goes boom and kills us all. A bomb that was made by someone that's pissed off because of you and your coven. If Torine is the big bad, I don't care! If she wants to cause you trouble after all this, I also don't care. The only thing that matters to me right now is making sure the bomb doesn't go off and Torine is the only way to do that. You can get on board with the plan, or you can step aside."

Sebyl parted her lips to speak, but I held up my hand, silencing her. "And as Mom pointed out, you no longer speak for the High Coven. We're going to put this up for a vote and for once, every witch in this damn townhouse will get a say." I clicked my teeth together. "Anyone have a problem with that?"

As I easily predicted, literally no one except Sebyl had a problem with it. Whatever issues the high priestess had with Torine, it wasn't a big enough deal for the other coven witches to want to die over. I wished I could say my heart wasn't pitter-pattering with joy over putting Sebyl in her place, but I'd be lying. Even now, riding the night train to the other side of Stamwick where Torine lived, I was jumping out of my skin.

The train bumped and groaned over the tracks as we sped through the underground. Deep down, my stomach twisted and turned, my back pressed to River's chest as we huddled under the flickering overhead light of the train car. It was late enough that the car was mostly abandoned with only the two of us, Beatrix, Rhiamon, and Peyton, taking up space. Several shadowers asked to join when I told Peyton where we were headed, but she suggested they sit tight. The last thing we needed was to scare Torine off by showing up with a party crew in tow.

We needed the witch docile and willing to help.

The brakes hissed, and I pressed my palm against the side window to keep from toppling forward. A few seats over, Peyton bounced up and down, her entire fist in her mouth as she chewed her nails down to the core. Everyone was a nervous wreck.

Torine was our last shot at surviving.

As the doors slid open, I checked my phone and the timer app I installed. Twenty-two hours. Shit.

"It's a few blocks down from the station," Rhiamon said. Her long leather coat swayed behind her, and I caught flashes of silver from the sword strapped to her body.

I quirked a brow, tilting my head to the side.

"The coven knows all," Rhiamon whispered, then

winked. "Just because Torine was banished doesn't mean we stopped keeping tabs."

Acid filled my mouth. Even when you left the High Coven, you never really got away.

We cleared the stairs leading up to street level in record time, my eyes shifting left and right to make sure no one followed us. Solen mentioned Vic was worried Cathan might be onto our lead and want to beat us to the witch, so it was best to stay alert. Unfortunately, I had about five hours of sleep spread over days and I was seriously feeling the lag. I pinched my cheeks, rubbing my blood-shot eyes. Less than a full day. I only had to last less than a full day and then... well, I'd either get to sleep or I'd be sleeping for eternity. Either way, I'd be well rested.

Cringing at my own terrible joke, I tightened my grip on River's hand and moved my sore legs. We turned down a small residential street, and I had to do a double-take when Rhiamon pointed her long finger at one of the tiny bungalows.

"This place?" I asked. "Really?"

Torine's house was the exact opposite of what I would imagine a witch's home to look like. Even Miss Broussard's apartment over the magic shop appeared more otherworldly than the plain beige box we were quickly approaching.

"Yo, there aren't even wards on here," Peyton noted, studying the front door. "Like anyone could walk right in. Awkward."

My thigh muscles tightened. She was right. Something wasn't adding up here and I couldn't quite put my finger on it. Maybe Rhiamon got the address wrong because no way would a witch—especially one banished by the High Coven —would keep herself exposed this way. We inched closer to the entrance, my eyes desperate to adjust to the lack of light. Did someone turn off all the lights on the porch, or was Torine not home? Dropping River's hand, I took one long stride to get in front of the door.

"What is it, babe?"

"I'm not sure," I whispered. My palms brushed over the door and I scowled. It was rougher than I expected, almost like... My nose hiked up, and I took a long whiff. "Do you smell that? It smells like—"

"Camping," River said. "Fuck."

I turned on the flashlight on my phone and pointed it at the doorframe, the blood leaving my body. The entire front door was burned to a crisp. I cast a side glance at River, then motioned for the rest of our group to stay quiet. With a trembling hand, I touched a finger to the door handle and winced. Still hot. Slowly, I peeled off my scarf and wrapped it around the handle, careful not to get scorched. As I twisted, the creaking of the door made my insides slosh around and my heart dropped to the floor when we entered the house.

In the middle of the burnt-down living room stood Cathan. Seven fire fae surrounded him, flames dancing on their fingers. My father's face twisted, lips peeling back to a sneer. "Took you long enough, daughter of mine."

Chapter
Twenty-seven

Billie

As quickly as possible, I surveyed the room we stood in. Unlike the front of the house, there was a lot more magic crammed into the inside of Torine's home. When my eyes adjusted to the low light, I spotted shelves full of crystals and herbs and several cauldrons in varying sizes scattered throughout the large room. To my right and behind Cathan and his merry men of misery was a long hallway, which I assumed led to the bedrooms. From here, I could see into the small kitchen on the left; in it, more magical items lined the counters like they had been abandoned mid-use.

My throat dried up. "Where the hell is Torine?"

"You didn't think I'd make it this easy, did you?" Cathan sneered.

I balled my hands into fists and called on my shadow magic. My knees knocked with the pressure building inside me and when I forced my arms toward Cathan, darkness exploded around us. The shadows stormed the living room and rushed for the fae bastard, picking up speed quickly.

With one flick of his wrist, Cathan blocked the attack, the nasty smile never leaving his face.

The sound of bones cracking vibrated through the room, and I felt the air whoosh by me as River's wolf leapt toward Cathan. Two fire fae jumped in front to intercept him with balls of flame at the ready. River's massive fur-covered body slammed into one of them and rolled on the ground. Instantly, the second fae jumped into the action. I watched, my eyes wide, as the three fought. I was about to jump in to help when the entire house started to shake. Beneath my feet, the wooden planks of the floor cracked, and pieces of sub-floor jutted out at sharp angles.

I tore my gaze from River, gasping. On either side of me crouched Rhiamon and my mom. Their palms squeezed into the floor and their heads lolled backward as they summoned the Earth elements under us.

Smiling, I dared to sneak a peek at Cathan. He didn't move, but I noticed the stupid grin he sported before vanish, replaced with a look of utter irritation. *You haven't seen anything yet!* I glanced over my shoulder at Peyton. "Call for backup!"

"Already done, ma'am!" my best friend replied, waving her cellphone in the air.

Nodding, I broke into a sprint and crossed the living room, closing the distance between Cathan and me. I could hear Peyton on my heels as she ran, and the sound of a body dropping echoed near me. In the corner of my eye, I watched Peyton slam the heels of her palms into one fae's chest, and the moron fell down like an overfull trash bag. Lesson to learn, kids. Always bring a Soul Sucker to a gunfight.

Lips peeling back from my teeth, I took the last few steps, my magic shooting out from my fingers. The shadows slammed into the fae blocking Cathan from view and her feet slid across the shaking floor. I continued to pump more shadows into her body, walking closer and closer with each push of energy. The fae's yellow eyes bulged out and she let out a guttural scream before her body collapsed in on itself. I pulled my magic back in and she fell down with a loud thud.

Then, I faced my prick of a father.

Cathan raised his hands and my arms jumped up instinctively, shadows swarming around me. Instead of blasting me with his power, he curled his lips and clapped. Slowly. What a tool. I shook my head and started to collect whatever energy I had left in me to throw at the monster, when bodies rushed into the room from the distant hallway. More fire fae than I could count crowded the living room; my veins sizzled.

We were outnumbered. By a lot.

Not far from where I stood, I heard River growl and Peyton curse. The ground shook harder as my mom and Rhiamon pumped more of their magic out, trying to throw the fae off balance.

I snapped my jaw tightly, running my tongue against the roof of my mouth. "Where is SHE! If she's dead, I'm going to end you!" I roared.

"Tsk, tsk, tsk." Cathan wagged his nasty little finger. "I'm not making it easy for you. Accept your fate, daughter of mine. Say your goodbyes."

My body moved before I could stop it and I lunged for his throat. As I zoomed through the air, I stretched my fingers out. I was going to choke the life out of the bastard. Something hard slammed into my side and I went catapulting over. Pain shot through me. I winced as I crashed into the wall head first.

Vision flickering, I dragged myself up to stand, searching the room for the fae that pushed me over. There were so many of them, I couldn't spot the assailant, though I noticed three guys widening their stances as they readied to come at me. My hands fisted, and I blew a stray hair away from my eyes. *Try it and die, boys.*

Before they had a chance to move, a thought popped into my head and I gulped. "Why are you doing this?" I asked Cathan. "If the bomb goes off, you die too. Everyone here will perish."

I didn't know why it didn't occur to me before. Perhaps it was the adrenaline that'd been driving me the last few days or the fear of losing everyone I loved, but I never even gave it a second thought. Why would Cathan create a bomb if it was going to kill every magical creature on Earth? At the start, I assumed he made a weapon that would exclude the fae, but now that I stood here, it finally dawned on me. It couldn't. All our magic, everything we were, came from fae magic. If the bomb targeted magical energy, it would have to include the fae. I eyed my father through thin slits.

Was this man really going to sacrifice himself to prove a point?

The blood in my veins cooled. I shivered. "You have a way out, don't you?"

"Bravo, daughter of mine."

Hope fluttered in my chest. The only way for Cathan to escape would be to leave Earth before it went off. He knew how to open the portal. We could use his escape to help us. If I played this right, Cathan could lead us to the portal site he planned to use, and once he left this realm, we'd transfer the energy from the bomb to Faerie. Two birds, one stone. Or one portal, one bomb in our case. There was no room for error with this plan. I already sent word to Logan to be ready, I only hoped he could cross the fae over and fight off Cathan at the same time. Our main concern was for Torine to do whatever she had to for the transfer. It could work, but the timing would have to be perfect, and most importantly, we needed Torine. Alive.

My body froze as I counted the fire fae in the room.

Why bring so many of them here? This must have been all the fae that followed Cathan to Earth. Why would he risk his entire line of defense on one witch? Even if Vic's hunch was right and Torine could transfer the bomb's energy, we needed to open another portal to succeed, and Cathan was the only one who knew how.

Unless...

"Torine is alive!" I yelled out to the others. "She can open the portal! We need to find her now!"

My body ached from the pain of being knocked down, but I fought through it. Gathering all the energy I had left in my bones, I cast my father a steely gaze and spread my arms wide. Then I let loose of every shadow I could summon.

As the room turned to pitch black around us, I couldn't help but laugh.

Chapter
Twenty-eight

Savannah

"Move it or lose it, people! You in the red! Take only what you can carry. You can't bring your whole damn house with you!" I spat out commands right, left, and center at the herd of fae filling the palace. There were so many of them, they started to spill out into the front gardens and some already began to crowd the bridge.

Holy crap. That's a lot of people.

For some reason, I didn't expect there to be so many, which was hella dumb since we were relocating all of Faerie. Literally everyone and their mother were here. I shielded my eyes from the overhead sun and peered down at the crowd. No sign of the fire fae.

When Solen dreamed-walked his butt back over and told us Billie said to get ready, we sent out some of the neutral representatives to share the news with the fire fae. Logan hoped they would see reason and join the rest in crossing over once the portal was open, but I wasn't so sure. Those fools have been throwing for control of the realm since Cathan hightailed it back to Earth, and I doubted any of them were eager to leave. Especially since they wouldn't have a leg to stand on amongst all the humans.

Hiding was not exactly a fire fae specialty. Those stubborn bastards were all about showy power—something they'd have very little of back on Earth. At least, if what Victoria said was true.

According to the witch, with the connection between Faerie and Earth gone, the fae's energies would be the main source of keeping magic alive. With every witch and shadower siphoning their magic, the fae would not be as powerful as they were in their own realm. Especially since it was Faerie that was providing them with that power. I wondered if anyone bothered to explain to these people what they were getting themselves into.

I reached down to help a young fae secure a pack to her back, but as I stretched out the straps, the ground shook violently beneath my feet. The girl's tiny fingers gripped mine, and I hoisted her up on my side, trying to stay balanced. A loud explosion pierced the air and my ears perked, following the sound to somewhere beyond the bridge. In the distance, the stone structure spanning between the palace and forest shook, and screams rose from the crowd upon it. Clinging to me for dear life, the girl started to wail, and my ears popped from the high-pitched cry. I turned around and around, finally spotting her parents in the panicked group of fae near me.

Handing the child off, I pushed my way through a sea of fae, looking for Logan.

"Bloody hell, mate! Make room!"

There he is. My feet pounded the purple dirt as I rushed through the front gardens toward Logan's voice. Fae were everywhere. In their panic from the explosion, they ran in all directions. Some searched for cover while others only paced around like wild animals woken from a deep slumber. I squeezed myself between bodies, trying to clear as much ground as possible without getting trampled. A grouping of fire sprites slammed into my face and I swung my arms around, careful not to squish them. Or worse, have one fly down my throat because my stupid mouth was wide open.

Clenching my jaw shut, I pushed my way to the outskirts of the crowd until I could finally see Logan in my sight line. His man-bun had come loose, and silver hair was flying all around him as he cursed and muttered while helping the fae get out of the way. For a second, he dipped down, and I lost him, then I noticed him pop back up, lifting a tiny, horned Earth fae onto his shoulders.

"Logan!" I yelled out.

His head swung around at the sound of my voice and we locked eyes. "Stay there, love! I'm coming your way!"

Even while carrying the child, Logan was much faster than me at clearing a path. It definitely helped that people got out of his damn way, some even bowing a little, when he passed. Must be nice to be king. I rolled my eyes and shoved a wide-ass shoulder out of my face. The fae it belonged to grumbled under his breath, then saw Logan approach and scurried away. My eye-roll intensified.

"What was that?" I asked, as Logan neared me. "Tell me that wasn't the bomb? Are we too late? Would we even feel it here if it went off?"

Logan held up a hand. "Whoa! Slow down. Not the bomb, and I'm not sure we'd feel it. I think the fire fae finally arrived. Bloody wankers."

My head spun, and I saw red.

"Are you freaking kidding me right now?!" I screeched.

"With everything that's going on, they're still having a pissing contest with you?"

"Looks like it."

A thick gust of wind swept over the crowd and I held onto Logan's arm for dear life. Above us, dark maroon clouds began to roll in, and the scowl on Logan's face deepened. "Those mutts somehow got the rogue air fae on their side."

All around us panic rose, and as the wind picked up, it only intensified. The sky got darker and darker and loud thunder hammered overhead. My eardrums burst, and I reached behind my back for the bow I carried, ready to show these morons the consequences of their own actions.

A strong hand gripped my arm, forcing it down. "It's fine, love. I got this," Logan said. He reached up and picked up the fae boy, handing him over. "See if you can find his parents."

"What are you going to do?"

Logan smirked. "Reason with the sodding devils."

With that, he ducked out of sight and disappeared into the crowd. I gave the boy a reassuring nod and asked, "Let's see if we can find your mom and dad, yeah?" Tears glistened in his eyes, but he blinked them away. Tough little fella.

One foot out, I started to make my way back into the sea of fae at the base of the bridge when the ground rumbled under me again. My eyes jerked past the bridge to see if there was another attack, but all I saw was the biggest group of fire and air fae standing guard on the opposite side of the ravine. My teeth ground together so hard, I was pretty sure they turned to dust. What the hell was wrong with these fools? Were they truly willing to kill everyone in their pathetic attempt to gain power over Faerie? *News flash, morons! There won't be a Faerie for you to control soon.* So stupid.

The boy clung to me and I saw him stretch out a small green finger, pointing in the direction of the bridge. I half expected to see more fire fae, but what I saw instead made my stomach churn. A massive tree root burst from the ground, shaking it under my feet again. So, that was what I felt last time. More roots pierced the ground and shot up into the sky, intertwining as they climbed higher. At their base stood Waverly with several Earth fae, their eyes closed and their palms dancing in slow movements before them. "They're directing the roots!" I yelled out.

In my arms, the little boy nodded.

I watched, mesmerized, as more roots were pulled from the ground and into the sky. What were they doing? Forming a barrier? No. Not a barrier. From here, it almost looked like—

"Please tell me it's not what I think it is," I whispered.

It was definitely what I thought it was.

Moments after the roots settled into what appeared to be a creepy-ass ladder, Logan's face popped up from the crowd. His hair blew in the wind that continued to gain speed as he climbed up the root-ladder, all the way to the top. When he reached it, Waverly waved her slender hand and one root separated from the rest to wrap over Logan's waist, securing him in place. Then the entire contraption shot forward.

It happened so quickly, I yelled out in a panic.

One second Logan was standing on our side of the ravine, and the next he was hanging over the bridge, flying closer to the fire and air fae. In the distance, shouts sounded, and I saw flashes of red as the idiots threw up their dumb fireballs. I wanted to warn Logan, but he seemed completely oblivious to the dangers below him.

Instead, he cleared his throat and started to yell.

"I know you're upset! And I know you want me out of your bloody hair," he roared. *Interesting start.* "I'm not sure how much Waverly's group shared with you, but you need to realize that I'm on your side."

"You're on the side of the witches!" someone yelled from below. "A traitor! Not a king!"

If Logan was bothered by their words, he didn't show it. "I never wanted to be your king, but now that I'm in this position, I'm doing what is best for everyone. Or did you want someone like Cathan back on the throne?"

Silence.

Morons.

"As I said," Logan continued. "Look around you! No one wants to leave and yet look at all your mates. They are picking up their lives and finding whatever spot of sodding bravery they have left—they're working together! It's going to be different, that I won't deny. Earth is nothing like this place. But it has its advantages."

"Like what? The witches?"

Logan shook his head. "Like a fresh start. You're here, in this realm, not by choice, but because long ago, witches made sure you couldn't leave. Were those witches twats? Yes. Are some of them of the same mindset today? Also yes."

My eyes widened. What point was he trying to make here?

"But guess what?" Logan said. "Not all the fae are prime examples of teamwork. I mean, look at right now—you lot are literally standing in the way of your kind surviving, and all you see is your hatred for me. Are you willing to damn all the fae to put me in my place? Because while I can't guarantee that you will have the same life on Earth as you have here, what I *can* guarantee is that this realm will be gone. And soon. There will not be a Faerie, not if my sister is as powerful as I know she is. She will find a way to save everyone, fae and witch and shadower alike. Because, if you can believe it, some witches actually care about others."

He looked down at the wall of people beneath him and flicked his fingers. Dark shadows danced on his skin and his lavender eyes deepened in color. My thighs got tingly from seeing Logan in his element. I shook myself back to reality. *Focus, girl. Geez.* Logan's shadows continued to swirl around him as he said, "The way I see it, you have two options. Keep up this nonsense and we can battle it out until none of us are left standing, or—" he smiled, "—join your fellow fae and do what's right by them."

There was an eery silence on the opposite end of the bridge and my eyes narrowed while Logan's smirk widened. "Wanna know what the upside of leaving really is?" he asked, chuckling. "Once we're back on Earth, I go my own way and you go yours. There are no kings there. You will be free!"

Cheers erupted from our side of the bridge as I looked around, seeing the fae as they were for what felt like the first time. Everything Logan said was right. Witches or not, these people could be whatever they wished on Earth. They could live wherever they wanted, do as they pleased; they could finally have a life outside of this beautiful prison.

I stretched my gaze past Logan and to the angry mob, which looked a lot less mad right now. Some of their fires vanished, and while they continued to stand guard, I could see their posture change. They were coming around. Above us, the clouds dispersed as the air fae chose a side. I watched a few bodies shift, making room for our passage across the bridge.

Atop the root-ladder, Logan twisted around, his eyes finding mine. He winked and my shoulder hunched. I knew Logan would never admit this, but he was a real leader. I smiled, flashing him a thumbs up. Logan Green was a damn king whether he liked it or not, and he was all mine.

The fae continued to cheer as Waverly used her magic to lower him back down. As soon as his feet hit the ground, he was rushed by hundreds of fae. Joy spread over the palace for the first time in what seemed like decades, and I gazed at the little boy in my arms, watching him wipe his eyes.

Well, maybe not all mine. I glanced at Logan's uncomfortable face as he was engulfed in fae bodies, and laughed. I supposed I didn't mind sharing him for a little while longer.

Chapter
Twenty-nine

River

*B*illie's shadows engulfed us; the entire room faded to black. I shook my snout back and forth and stomped my front paws to clear the darkness that swallowed me up. Snarling, I tried to find Billie, but I couldn't see anything at all. The wolf whined as I made a second attempt to regain some vision.

Fuck this, I thought and shifted back to human form.

Doing a quick check of my arms, I noted that our bond marks remained still; Billie wasn't in any immediate danger. Good. Somewhere in the room, a pained cry rang out, and the sound of a body hitting the floor filled my ears. I cut my way through Billie's shadows and bee-lined toward the yell I heard. My foot caught on something and my body wobbled seconds before I lost all balance. Whatever tripped me took me down hard. My nose hit the hardwood first and a sharp pain spread from it to the back of my head. I ran my tongue along the top lip, the taste of iron making me gag.

Scowling, I pressed my hand to my face, pulling it away wet. *Great, I think I broke my damn nose.* I cursed, feeling around for whatever it was I tripped on. Blood dripped down my face and I hiked up my chin to keep from tasting it again. It was a pointless task and soon I was pretty much choking it down. So gross. I coughed, hands feeling the floor near my legs. My fingers touched something hot and fleshy and I pulled them back, then reached out again. This time, I felt a hard object that curved outward.

Horns.

I must have tripped over the fae Billie took down with her magic.

A smile tugged at my lips and it made my broken nose scream in agony. I cursed, forcing my legs to straighten so I could climb to stand. There was a commotion to my left, and I braced for impact, but one never came.

"Babe, not that I don't love whatever is happening here," I said into our bond. *"But do you think you could tone it down a little? I'm falling face over ass back here."*

A chuckle shook my body and in seconds, some of the shadows lifted, allowing me to see a bit more of the room. Man, what a sight it was. In the span of what felt like mere moments, Billie managed to turn the tables around in our favor. The spot in the living room where Cathan and his pathetic fae stood before was now empty, and my eyes traveled to the walls where my mate pinned down five of the fae with her magic, two males and three females. They wriggled under the hold of the shadows, but each time they moved, Billie's magic tightened around their necks and chests. Their faces turned red, then blue, then white as they slowly stopped breathing. When their arms dropped to the sides, Billie's shadows retreated, and the sound of bodies crashing to the floor filled the room.

I looked at her face and stumbled back as two glowing orbs stared back at me.

Billie was all up in her shit now.

A groan sounded behind me and I spun around to see Peyton take down two giant fae dudes with only the touch of her fingers. Even from here, I could feel her power in the air. For all her perkiness, I tended to forget how dangerous Peyton was. How deadly.

To my right, Beatrix and Rhiamon sliced and diced their way through a crowd of angry fire fae that kept coming. I wasn't sure where the hell all these ass-hats were showing up from, but the witch's bungalow started to resemble a magician's hat. You get a fae, and you get a fae, and you get a fae...

Focus, River.

I scolded myself and turned my attention back to the living room and the reason we were here. We had to find Torine. When we arrived and saw Cathan, I was sure the witch was dead and that without her, we would be soon, too. But Billie seemed convinced she was alive. Better: that she could open the portal. A win for the good guys. I shook myself off and started for Billie when her voice penetrated our bond.

"I'm going for Cathan. Can you find Torine and keep her safe?"

I nodded, heading for the long hallway leading away from the center of the battle.

"Um, babe?"

I turned toward her. *"What's up?"*

"Maybe the wolf can handle this."

Billie nudged her chin in my direction and I followed her eyes down my naked body. Shit. Right, I didn't bring spare clothes with me. Acting fast to avoid giving everyone more of a show than they were already getting, I called for the wolf, shifting faster than I ever have before. My paws stomped down on the floor. I shook out my fur, sharp eyes trained on my main objective. Make it to the hallway... find Torine.

The wolf yelped as I took off in a sprint.

Shouts and grunts continued in my wake. I heard light steps gaining speed behind me. I glanced over my shoulder, flipping back around when I realized it was only Billie. She kept up, jogging fast to stay in line with the wolf's trajectory. It made sense she followed—chances were, if Torine was in one of these rooms, Cathan wouldn't be far behind.

"Left!" Billie shouted at my back.

I skidded to a slower pace and rammed my body to the left, my side hitting the hallway wall. On my right, the flash of lightning zooming by blinded me for a moment, and I had to shake my head to clear my spotted vision. The wolf whined at the fatal hit we dodged by mere inches. I looked back, past the length of the hallway and into the living room, where Beatrix was kicking some serious ass with lightning she summoned out of thin air. Her hair whipped around her as she twisted in a circle, slamming her magic into every fae that got in her way. From here, she looked so much like Billie, it was frightening. "Sorry!" Beatrix yelled out, while continuing to kick ass.

Bristling, I nudged my snout in the direction of the first door coming up and trotted forward with Billie on my heels. Standing on my hind legs, I scratched at the door, my sharp nails slipping off the handle.

"I got it," Billie said, turning the knob.

The door flew open as Billie threw her shadows at it. They swirled around the room, clearing it of any danger while the two of us huddled in the frame. When Billie pulled her shadows back, they revealed a very empty, very unassuming bedroom. There was a large window on the far wall and a canopied, king-sized bed against it. The bed covers were a mess, and when I looked around the room, I noticed a broken picture frame lying at the base of the only dresser in sight.

Billie must have come to the same conclusion as I did. "This is where they snatched her."

Pressing my nose to the floor, I whined and inhaled sharply. At this point, I could recognize Cathan's stench anywhere and when I got a big whiff of it, the wolf snarled. Warm saliva dripped from my open jaw as I scratched at the floor, letting Billie know I picked something up. Separating Cathan's gross scent from the rest of the room, I zeroed in on another fragrance. This one was more whimsical and had notes of... I couldn't quite put my finger on it.

"There's something else here, but I can't place it. It might be—"

"Rose, frankincense, and dragon's blood," Billie said. She held up a leather pouch dangling off a long, silver chain. "Protection spell. Torine tried to fight back."

I glanced at the door, my nose high up in the air. *"I can follow it."*

Bolting from the room, I stayed on the scent, following it all the way down the hallway to another door. Unlike the others, this one was made entirely of brass and had intricate runes carved into a circle in its center. I let out a low growl and pointed my nose in its direction.

"She must have a safe room in the house," Billie noted. She reached for the handle and gave it a twist, but nothing happened. "Ugh! It's locked. Hang on."

Her fingers twitched, and she reached into her shirt, pulling out a bright yellow crystal. "Always come prepared."

One hand on the crystal and one on the handle, Billie whispered something under her breath and I heard the click of a lock. This time, when she twisted the door handle, it opened. Before us were a set of stairs leading down into a basement. We exchanged twin looks of worry before charging down. My paws pushed off, and I cleared two steps at a time, landing on the bottom in record time. A second later, Billie appeared beside me. The basement was pitch black and smelled of herbs and something akin to vinegar. It took a moment for my eyes to adjust, and when they did, I planted both my paws on the concrete floor, standing directly in front of Billie.

In the dark of the underground bunker, Cathan's teeth glowed as his wolfish grin widened. His wretched eyes narrowed on us and he reached out beside him, yanking something out of the deep shadows into his chest. No, not something. *Someone.*

Cradled into his chest was a woman I did not recognize. Her hair was tied into a messy bun of tight, thin braids, and she had smudges of dark liner around her eyes. Her lips were painted a deep shade of purple, and she wore a long, layered silk dress adorned with hundreds of tiny crystals. Despite the situation, Torine looked like she was utterly bored. This witch was the real deal.

"Let her go!" Billie roared.

Cathan only laughed. His arms curled in farther and his slimy lips twirled up at the edges. Something glimmered in his hand, and I noticed the knife he held for the first time. He pressed it deeper into Torine's neck and she flinched as a drop of blood rolled down her skin. Iron filled the air, and I pressed my paws deeper into the floor as the wolf let out a loud howl.

"Tell your dog to stay," Cathan warned. "Or she dies."

"Bullshit," Billie countered.

The monster dug the edge of the blade deeper in and Torine's eyes widened. "I am not playing, daughter of mine."

It seemed Billie was also not playing because I heard her yell "Duck!" right before she fired her magic at the ex-king's face. Torine whipped out of Cathan's grasp, the knife slicing across her neck. She pressed her palm to her skin and twirled out of the way as Billie's shadows circled Cathan. My mate's eyes lit up and painted the basement in a bright, white glow. I looked around, skimming past the etchings on the walls. The entire bunker we stood in was covered in them and in its center, directly under Cathan, a circle was cast out of pure silver.

Seriously, this witch was not messing around.

I shook myself out, refocusing my attention on Billie and Cathan. She had him good, and I was pretty sure she was going to take the final fatal blow at any moment.

"Are you truly going to kill your own father?" Cathan gasped.

Billie shot out one more shadow and it wrapped over his mouth, shutting him up. *She sure is going to kill, you prick.* I snapped my jaw shut and stomped my front paws into the ground. *"Get him, babe."*

Except Billie didn't. My eyes darted to hers, and I saw the briefest hint of hesitation flash across her face. It was enough to buy Cathan time. His arms slashed across Billie's shadows, and he whipped his hands forward, releasing his own magic. Dread settled in my gut and the wolf let out a high-pitched whine as I watched Cathan's magic barrel straight for Billie. Not waiting, I gathered all the strength I had in my body, pushed off my hind legs and leapt into the air.

I soared through the room, throwing myself between Billie and Cathan's shadows.

"River, NO!"

My body collided with the magic, and pain, unlike any other, ripped through my chest. The force of the hit catapulted me backward and my back slammed into the back wall so hard, blinking lights appeared in my periphery. I slid to the floor, dropping down faster, faster, faster. Then, the noise in the bunker went away and my vision flooded with black. I shut my eyes, forgetting where I was. In my nostrils, the smell of blood and burning flesh tickled my hairs as the world shut down around me.

Chapter
Thirty

Billie

*R*iver's large, gray wolf crumbled like a marionette. His ribcage moved up and down, and I swallowed hard, relieved to see him breathing. Around his limp body, Cathan's shadows swirled, and if I didn't know better, I'd have thought they were doing a happy dance. My head swiveled toward my jerk of a father. *I'm going to make you pay.*

Above us, the house shook violently and my stomach pitched as the basement floor vibrated under my feet. Rubble fell from the ceiling. I ducked out of the way as a splintered piece of wood came crashing down beside me. Less than twenty feet away, Cathan swerved to avoid another broken beam. Eyes darting to the far corner where Torine crouched, I made sure the witch was alive, then refocused my attention back on Cathan. His palms were pressed together as if in prayer, and I watched as he gathered the magic within him, readying for a hit. My thoughts ran a mile a minute, formulating a plan.

I narrowed my eyes and called forth the shadows,

building a wall in front of me the color of night. With my body hidden from sight, I walked toward Cathan, all while continuing to feed shadows into my self-made barricade. Slowly, without attracting attention, I pulled out the amethyst pendant from inside my shirt and wrapped my fingers over it. My eyes could barely see through the small slit between the shadows, but I caught a glimpse of Cathan going on the defensive. He widened his stance and flipped his palms, two dark balls levitating inches above his skin. Good. Let him think I'm coming for him with my spirit magic.

When I cleared half the space between us, I stopped and pushed one arm out, directing the shadows to fly for him. As I predicted, Cathan used his magic to block the attack. While he was busy fighting, I threw out my other hand and called for the wind. It rushed from my fingers toward my cowardly father, catching him off guard. The gust of wind slammed into his chest and threw him backward, his feet grazing the floor as he rushed through the air.

My eyes flashed to his, then to the metal pipe protruding from the wall behind him.

A guttural scream pierced the basement as Cathan's shoulder collided with the pipe. The metal slashed through his flesh, shooting out the other side. Cathan screamed again, squirming against the wall and trying to free himself.

Before he could escape, I pointed a finger to my right, the wind picking up the splintered piece of wood that almost killed me earlier. Flipping it in the air, I pointed the damn thing like a stake and shot it at Cathan's other shoulder. He screamed and my stomach turned as dark blood stained his white shirt.

Cathan thrashed against my restraints, but it was a futile task. I had him pinned. Literally.

Pace slow and steady, I made my way toward him, stopping a few feet in front of his ashen face. I glanced in River's direction. "You shouldn't have done that."

The steps behind me creaked, and I looked over my shoulder. Feet clambered down into the basement—one set, two sets, three sets. The rest of our party showing up to help River and me. I kept my eyes on Cathan and waved for them to stand back. "I got this," I growled out. "Someone check on River."

"On it, B!" Peyton yelled out, and I heard her rush to my mate.

"We need him," Rhiamon warned, sensing my need to blow Cathan to smithereens. "He's the only one that knows where the bomb is."

My lips pursed, then flattened into a thin line. Teeth grinding, I flicked my gaze to Torine. "I don't think that's true." I frowned. "You're the one that helped him create this bomb in the first place, aren't you?"

"I did."

My chest tightened. "How could you? Did you know he kept innocent fae imprisoned on Earth for centuries, waiting to fulfill this heinous plan when he decided it was time for it?" My mouth was suddenly full of saliva. I spat at my feet, anger for Torine coursing through me. "What the hell were you thinking?"

The witch froze, her sapphire eyes lowering. I watched as she brought her knees into her chest and squeezed. "It was a long time ago," she whispered. "I was a different person then. An angry person."

"Pathetic," Rhiamon hissed between clenched teeth.

At that, the witch's shoulders straightened, and she pointed a crooked finger at the priestess. "It was *you* I was angry with," she bit out. "Don't claim innocence in this. If your coven didn't banish me, the fae king never would have sought me out to help him. He had plans for this bomb for centuries, all he needed was a witch mad enough to bring it to life. Until you four, the High Coven was united. How many witches do you think are out there who would do anything to get back at you and your sisters?"

No one answered. Mostly because she had a pretty good point. There was a time when I was so pissed off with the High Coven, there was no telling how far I would have gone to hurt them. If a smooth-talking slime ball like Cathan showed up, promising everything I wanted in exchange for a small favor, I wasn't sure what I would have done. I looked back at Rhiamon, her chin tucked into her chest and her eyes cast downward. It seemed the high priestess was coming to the same conclusion.

"Where is it?" I asked Torine. "Where is the bomb?"

Her lips parted, and she said, "It's the—"

Inky black magic surrounded her and poured into her mouth. Torine's eyes bulged, and she threw her head back, hitting it against the concrete wall behind her. I glanced at Cathan, noticing the fingers on his limp hands moving slightly. The bastard was still trying to get in my way. My eyes flared and my blood turned to ice. In seconds, I cleared the distance between us. Arms shooting up, I forced my magic upward, wrapping it around one of the large beams overhead. A growl vibrated my chest as my rage overtook me. "Let her go or I swear, I will make this more painful than it has to be."

Cathan's lips parted, drops of blood speckled on their

edges. He sucked in a shuddering breath and said, "Finally, the daughter I've always wanted."

On my right, I saw Torine shake her head violently, and I gagged in my mouth. This piece of garbage. This waste of space. I had enough of Cathan and his games, enough of his viscous, evil plans. The monster trapped before me didn't think I had it in me to kill my own father. Well, he was about to find out how wrong he was. My lips tugged at the edges and I flashed Cathan my teeth.

"I hope you rot in hell," I said.

Then I tore the metal beam from the ceiling and brought it down on the fae king's head.

Chaos erupted around me. The house shook overhead as more beams began to loosen. I heard my mom shout for everyone to get up the stairs. Twisting around, I waited until Peyton and Rhiamon dragged River's wolf body half way up, then bolted for Torine. As I passed Cathan, or what was left of him, I tried not to look. Not only because I was pretty certain what I would see would haunt me for the rest of eternity, but because I couldn't afford to get up in my feels right now. *Get out, then deal with it.* I tore past the beam he lay under and landed on my knees next to the witch. With Cathan dead, his magic no longer held her, but she looked like she was going to pass out any second.

I threw one of her arms over my shoulder. "Can you walk?"

She nodded, standing up with my help. We ran for the stairs as beams and pieces of the house came crashing down around us. Someone called my name from the upper level and I didn't bother answering. My boots hit the steps hard as I dragged Torine behind me, trying to clear the destruction before we were crushed. When I reached the top landing, I hauled the witch over and pushed her forward. Her body landed in a heap and I jumped out of the basement, flattening out beside her. Hands gripped my arms, and I felt myself being dragged forward. My eyes focused and refocused, black dots swarming my vision.

Suddenly, the air was fresher. My back flattened out. I stared up, seeing a starry sky above me. Slowly, I got up on my elbows, looking around. Torine's house was completely destroyed. There was some semblance of a structure, but for the most part, it seriously looked like someone took a bulldozer to it.

I hope she wasn't planning on selling.

Shaking my head, I worked against my own body to stand up, turning my attention to everyone else in the front yard. Around us, the barrier Rhiamon cast stood strong, and I was grateful we didn't have Torine's human neighbors to worry about. At least not yet. I was sure there would be questions in the morning when people woke up and saw the hot mess that was the witch's bungalow.

My eyes found Peyton's, and I rushed toward her, dropping to my knees by River. My palm rested on his fur, feeling his chest go up and down slowly.

"He's okay," Peyton said. "Just out of it."

"Thank the Goddess." I turned around, searching the front yard until I spotted Torine. As quickly as my broken body would allow it, I walked toward her. When I reached the witch, confusion set in. Instead of looking relieved that we survived, Torine appeared to be absolutely livid. I glanced from her to the rubble of her home. "Look, if this is about your house, we didn't have a choice. You saw what Cathan was planning. I—"

"You stupid, stupid girl!" Torine hissed. "You killed him!"

Come again? What the hell was she on about? Obviously, I had to kill Cathan—he was about to kill her. I looked at my mom, but she appeared as bewildered as me. "He was going to kill you," I told the witch.

"Better me than him."

I am confusion. "We need you to open the portal," I explained. "You can do that, right?"

Torine nodded, anger flashing over her features.

"Okay, so you open the portal and we get all the fae out. Then you transfer the energy from the bomb, since you know where it is, into Faerie, and we close it up. Easy peasy." I looked at her pissed-off face and added, "Victoria said you could do it. You're the energy transfer master, no?"

Torine mumbled something under her breath that I couldn't make out.

"What was that?"

The witch pinned me with a death glare and all the blood rushed from my body. "I said you're an idiot," she growled out. "There is no opening the portal without that fae bastard. When he made me create the damn thing, he added a loophole to make sure Faerie stays safe if he dies."

"But the portal... the energy transfer..."

"The portal is the bomb," Torine spit out. "You open the doorway to get the fae out, and we all die instantly."

Chapter Thirty-one

Billie

*N*onononono! How? Why? I didn't understand anything that just happened. My body was suddenly too heavy for my legs to hold up and I bent over my thighs, trying not to puke all over my boots. Behind me, something crashed. I cringed. More of Torine's house coming down to crush what was left of the fire fae and my father. To destroy our only way out.

Except that wasn't true, because the house wasn't what ruined everything, was it?

It was me.

I was the reason no one would survive the night.

Tears streamed down my face as I dropped to my knees, shaking. It was over. Everything we did, all we went through, was for nothing. In a few short hours, the bomb Cathan and Torine built was going to go off and everyone I loved would die. What the hell was the point of even trying to stop it? I was an idiot. I should have spent the last few days we had left with River, and Peyton, and my mom. With all of them.

Instead, I chased bullshit clues that got us nowhere in the end.

Why didn't I for a *second* consider that Cathan thought of everything?

He would never let us go and he would never quit. But I didn't think of it because all I could see was my chance to wipe the stain that was my father off the face of the Earth. And where did that leave me? I raked my hand through the grass, forming a tight fist and pulling some of it up. It left me on my knees in front of a busted bungalow with no hope and no time left.

This was all too much. I couldn't breathe. My throat closed up and my eyes felt like they were on fire. Something pressed on my chest and my heart slammed against my ribcage so fast I thought it might explode. *I'm having a heart attack. My damn heart is going to stop before I have a chance to say goodbye to people. I'm going to—*

"Babe?"

A hand squeezed my shoulder, and I stopped my sniveling long enough to look at River through a curtain of sweaty hair. I jumped up, wrapping my arms around him and pulling him close. "You're okay. You're okay. You're okay," I whispered into the crook of his neck.

"Only a scratch," River said, but I noticed him wince when I squeezed him tighter. "How are you?"

I pulled away from him. "I ruined everything," I said. "Cathan, he had a backup plan. We can't open the portal... we can't stop the bomb. It's over, River. There's no way out of this and it's all my fault."

River's arms wrapped around me and pulled me into him, gently kissing the top of my head. I inhaled his scent, savoring the moment that was likely our last. My fingers traced his muscular back, and I moved them downward, stopping when I felt fur. I pushed off slightly, my gaze traveling down River's body. A laugh bubbled out of me before I could stop it. "Um, what is that?" I pointed to the hot-pink, faux-fur scarf tied at his waist.

"Peyton's idea of pants," River said, shrugging.

My eyes flashed to my best friend.

"What?" Peyton yelled out. "It was my scarf or nothing. You're welcome!"

Burying my face in River's neck, I let go of a giggle and breathed him in. This might be the last time we get to spend this way... intertwined. Suddenly, the hairs on the back of my neck stood tall and my spidey senses came to life. We weren't alone. Someone else was coming.

I pushed myself away from my mate and caught my mother's gaze. She must have sensed the same thing I did, and held two large amber crystals, one in each hand. Beside her, Rhiamon drew her sword. My stomach turned, and I swallowed saliva, annoyed by the incoming interruption. What the hell did the fire fae want, and how many more of them were there? Surely with Cathan gone, they'd leave us alone. I really didn't want my last few hours alive to be spent fighting the ass-wipes. But a girl had to do what a girl had to do.

Taking a wide stance, I summoned the shadows from deep inside me and held them at my fingertips.

"Oh, for the love of the Goddess, put your magic away. It's only us."

My eyes bulged so far out of their sockets, I nearly lost them to gravity. Speed-walking down the street directly toward me was Sebyl. Behind her, the entire High Coven marched in unison, but that wasn't the shocking part. The part that all but unhinged me were the rogue witches and shadowers that marched alongside them. From here, I spotted Morgan and Lorelei chatting with two younger witches. Not far from them, Raiden led a large group of shifters that circled the group protectively, their bodies in constant motion and ready to shift if needed. My head did a double take, and I looked at River, mouthing, "What in the fresh hell?" before turning back to the group.

When their bodies filled the front yard, the place looked like a clown car.

Sebyl's thin lips puffed out, and she sucked in a ragged breath as she looked past my shoulder to what was left of Torine's house. "That is one way of handling the problem," the high priestess said.

"Did you...? Was that a...?" I stumbled on my words. "Are you actually making a joke right now? I get that you weren't here for the big show, but let me break it down for you. You're too late. The fight is over. I killed Cathan, and now we can't open the portal and save everyone because— news flash!—the portal is the bomb."

I think my voice must have gone up a couple of decibels because I saw Peyton wince a little from the corner of my eye. Whatever. I didn't care. The nerve of this woman! Showing up here way too late when she specifically said she didn't want anything to do with Torine in the first place. And why did she bring an army with her? How did she even get the shadowers to agree to come? None of this was making sense and yet the part that bothered me the most, the one that made me want to scratch Sebyl's eyes out, was her nonchalant kidding around when we were all about to die.

Seriously, what the hell, Sebyl?

The high priestess didn't entertain my freakout. Instead,

her gaze moved past me, briefly stopping on River's "pants," and flicking all the way to Torine. She tsked, a sly smile tugging at her red-painted lips. "I see we're back to not sharing everything we know again?" Sebyl cocked an eyebrow and Torine's jaw twitched. "I'm assuming by Billie's overreacting that you haven't yet told her the real reason for your banishment."

"What?" My head turned from Torine to Sebyl, then back again. "What is she talking about? Why did they cast you out, Torine?"

The witch sighed and brushed her hand over her dust-covered skirt. "Your friend, the one in Faerie, was right about my previous practices," she said.

"The energy transfers? I know! That's why we came here for your help." I looked back at Sebyl. "Vic said a witch got seriously hurt, and that's why you cast Torine out. What am I missing?"

Sebyl rubbed the bridge of her nose, her slim frame stiffening. "A witch didn't get hurt. A witch died. One of our high priestesses. Torine stole her magic and used it to create a weapon, one that was too dangerous for even the High Coven to want anything to do with."

Blinding pain knocked around in my head as I tried to piece Sebyl's story together. A dead high priestess? This must have been why Luna came on board to join Sebyl, Rhiamon, and Theodora. I was too young to remember it, but it made sense. That was why she was so much younger than the three. She started her journey as high priestess later than they did. I narrowed my eyes on Torine. She stole the magic from a high priestess? Why? Everyone knew that magic was the core of a witch's existence? Taking it would have catastrophic consequences, and in this case, deadly ones. I couldn't imagine a weapon could be worth—

My body froze. "You used her magic to make a bomb, didn't you?" I asked Torine. "The same kind of bomb we're dealing with now."

The witch nodded and tucked her chin into her chest.

Rage filled my belly. I leapt for her, ready to give the pathetic woman a black eye to match her black heart. Before I could make it far enough, River clasped my arms and pulled me back into him. His lips grazed my ear, and he whispered, "Think it over, babe. Think about what this means."

My mouth gaped.

"You're smarter than I gave you credit for," Sebyl told River. "Care to explain, Torine?"

"Can someone PLEASE get to the point?" Peyton whined.

Near to her, my mom said, "I second that request."

The headache I had before morphed into a full-on migraine, and I had trouble keeping my eyes in focus. If someone didn't fill me in ASAP, I was going to lose it. Luckily, I didn't have time for a panic attack because Torine finally decided to talk.

"In theory," she said, "if I have enough energy, I could fuse it with that of the bomb and contain it long enough to transfer it elsewhere."

"Like Faerie?" I asked.

The witch nodded. "But it won't be easy, and it might not work."

"Hey, if there's even a chance to save everyone, I think I can speak for us all when I say we're willing to take it." I looked around, but didn't see anyone object. "What about opening the portal? Will that not set the bomb off?"

"Not if I have the energy I need before we cast the opening."

I started to smile, then stopped. "You need another witch's magic to do this," I said. "That's the energy you keep talking about."

Another nod. *Effing great.*

There was a rustle of bodies and I felt a hand tug at my shoulder. I turned to face my mom, whose eyes were brimming with unshed tears. "Whatever you're thinking, don't," she said, her hand shooting up in the air. "You can take my magic. I give it freely."

"What? No way, Mom!" I yelped, twisting to face Torine. "Is there a way to do this without the risk of a witch dying?"

"I don't—"

"There is," Sebyl interrupted. She walked to stand by Rhiamon, and I noticed Luna trail beside her for the first time. The three exchanged looks and huddled closer together. "Long ago, before the High Coven became more civilized, when a witch acted against her sisters, there was a ritual performed. The coven stripped the witch of her magic before banishing her to the human world."

Wait, did she say the High Coven was civilized? I glanced at Peyton, who shrugged and made a cuckoo motion with her fingers. Stifling a laugh, I faced the high priestesses. "Can you perform it again?" I switched my attention to Torine. "If they can strip someone of magic, can you use that magic for your transfer?"

"Yes," she said.

"Okay, great. What about the portal? Can you open it?"

Torine let out a low whistle. "Kid, opening the portal will be the easiest thing I do tonight."

I brushed her cockiness off. Because gross.

"It's settled then," I said. "The High Coven will perform this weird little ritual and then Torine will use the energy transfer spell to get rid of the bomb once and for all. I need to get word back to Faerie. Hopefully Solen is waiting like I asked him to."

"Not so fast," Sebyl said. "We need to decide who is going to sacrifice their magic. This is not a simple ritual. It requires a price, one that is not easy to pay."

My heart jolted. "What price?"

"The witch's memory of magic existing. Since magic is the core of our being, once it is removed, the witch's memory of it vanishes," Sebyl explained. "She will never know of this world, of our world. The combined power of the coven can strip magic without the loss of a life, something Torine couldn't do on her own, but we cannot keep memories alive. It was why banishment always followed this ritual. Once performed, the witch will be nothing more than a human, forgetting everything she once did that touched the paranormal world."

Time slowed. I felt the front yard disappear, taking the arguments that rose with it. Around me, everyone yelled their opinion, but I couldn't hear them. I knew what I had to do. It was really nice that Mom offered to sacrifice her magic, but she only recently escaped a tiny cell in a magical prison where she had no magic at all. It wouldn't be fair to take away something she just got back. My chest ached at the thought of not remembering any of this. Would I remember my friends? River? A single tear rolled down my cheek, and I brushed it away. Around my waist, River's arms warmed my skin. I smiled.

"Are you sure?" he asked.

I nodded. "Yes. It has to be me. I have fae and witch magic. If anyone's power has a shot at ending this nightmare, it's mine."

"But what Sebyl said, it doesn't bother you? If your magic is who you are, won't you be missing a piece of yourself?"

I turned around in his arms and placed a soft kiss on his lips. "You are the core of who I am. And my mom. And Peyton." There was a loud howl from one of the wolves in the distance. I chuckled. "Even those guys. As long as I have you in my life, I'll have all the magic I need."

"It'll be hard to keep all this hidden from you."

Smiling, I kissed him again. "Hey, I had a ton of secrets when we first met, hunter. And look at us. Freaking thriving!"

River laughed, and the sound vibrated in his chest, shaking my whole body. I gave him a quick squeeze, then slithered out of his arms and walked toward Torine. The witch's eyes darkened, and I saw the glint of satisfaction cross her face. Before anyone could get in my way, I straightened my shoulders and said, "I'm ready. Take my magic, take my memories. Save the damn world."

Chapter
Thirty-two

Billie

*G*rass poked into the skin on the rear of my arms, and I tried not to move despite the growing itchiness I felt spreading through my body. My legs spread wide and my arms lay open wide inside the circle the High Coven cast around me. With time running out, we decided to perform the ritual right in Torine's front yard. Since the protective shield was still up, we had coverage from prying human eyes. And the entire coven was already here anyway, plus the rogue witches. Murmurs sounded around me. I closed my eyes, distancing myself from everyone else.

I had to concentrate to keep from losing my damn mind.

As far as I could tell, Torine couldn't guarantee where the portal would open in Faerie. A little while before I ended up in the middle of the circle and waiting to lose my magic, Luna cast a sleeping spell on my overstimulated butt so I could communicate with Solen. I was right and the fae was already waiting for me when I went night-night. The plan was for Torine to do her thing with my magic, then open the portal. I instructed Solen to get the fae spread out between all areas holding the most energy. Once the portal opened, we would need some time to get the energy transferred from the bomb, which should give everyone in Faerie a chance to make it to the portal site.

Goosebumps ran up and down my clammy skin.

We had only one shot at this, and we couldn't screw it up. Once the portal closed, the bomb would deploy and that would be the end of Faerie. I shut my lids tightly, fighting against tears. So much destruction because of one selfish person. I couldn't even begin to understand Cathan and his actions, but as much as I hated him, I was glad he wasn't here to see his home get destroyed. No one deserved that.

Not even Cathan.

"Ready?" Torine asked somewhere above me.

I gritted my teeth. "Yep."

"We'll be right here when it's over," my mom said, at the same time as River yelled, "You got this, babe!"

It took a bit of work to convince Beatrix that I had to be the one to give up her magic. Even as I lay here now and waited for the inevitable, I could feel her disappointment lingering in the air. Magic was everything to her, and it was everything to me for a long while. But I wasn't like my mom. Despite what happened between her and the High Coven, I saw how she was recently. How happy she'd been to be back around other witches and working alongside the high priestesses. No matter what Beatrix preached, the High Coven was her home. It was where she belonged.

Deep down, I knew she would find her way back there, with or without me.

And now with Theodora gone... who knew?

The situation with River would prove to be more difficult to maintain since he was the alpha of the wolf pack. Having to hide that would be tough, but I was sure we'd get through it. While Sebyl organized the ritual, River and I laid out some ground rules. Things he needed to hide from me, excuses he could give me for when it was time for him to be with the pack, things like that. We even pulled Peyton in to go over what to expect once my memory went.

In the end, there was only so much preparing we could do. For starters, no one actually knew what to expect, since the ritual hadn't been performed in ages. Then there was the time crunch we were under. The clock was ticking.

I opened my eyes and looked at the circle. Familiar faces crowded my vision, and I blinked rapidly, my wet lashes sticking together. All around me, witches I spent my life with held hands. Some smiled, and some were sobbing, the sadness of one of their own losing her magic overcoming them. I spotted Sebyl, Luna, and Rhiamon at the head of the circle.

"Thank you for everything you taught me," I said.

Sebyl nodded while the other two high priestess dabbed their eyes with the rear of their palms.

My eyes darted to my mother, who stood on the other side of Sebyl. "Mother-daughter movie night every Friday?"

"You bet!" she choked out. "And you better start thinking about colleges for next year."

I rolled my eyes and searched out Peyton in the crowd. It was awkward to say my goodbyes lying down, but I wasn't about to risk messing up the ritual, so I went with it. When I saw my best friend holding hands with Morgan next to Lorelei, I grinned like an idiot. "You better not ditch me," I teased.

"Are you kidding?" Peyton sniffled. "Who else am I going to gossip with? You're stuck with me for life, B. Obvi."

My head turned, the smell of grass filling my nostrils. On my arms, the mate marks swirled, their colors changing to the shades of aurora borealis I loved so much. My eyes found River's and butterflies fluttered in my stomach. I glanced down at our mate marks. *"I'm going to miss these."*

"They're only marks," River thought back to me. *"It's you and me. Forever."*

The tears I've been trying to hold back flowed down my face, and I rubbed at my eyes until they were bloodshot. Somewhere in the circle, Torine told us it was time to begin and my body stilled. This was it. Soon I would have no recollection of the spell, or any spells, for that matter. There would be no more shadow magic, no fae, or shadowers, no covens. I smiled. There would also be no running from Sebyl and no dealing with resistance politics. I would be a normal girl with a normal life. It was everything I'd ever wanted and yet...

I was seriously going to miss magic.

Before I could change my mind, I blinked away the last of the tears and closed my eyes, melting into the Earth beneath my body. Near to me, Torine started to chant and soon, every other witch in the circle joined in. The air cooled, and I felt the wind pick up all around me. The ground I lay on started to sink, swallowing me whole. I gripped onto the dirt, desperate to keep myself from being buried alive. My eyes flew open. I winced as the world spun out of control.

I needed to move.

I had to get up and shake off the increasing nausea swelling in my belly, but my bones were frozen in place.

Blinding pain ripped through my body and I threw my head back, my jaw stretching in a silent scream.

Then I was floating.

Gravity made me its bitch, and I rose above the Earth, my limbs falling uselessly to the sides. My limp body rose higher and higher until I was certain I would fly away. I was a party balloon with no strings. I was weightless. I was—

The surrounding air whooshed as I dropped back down, my back slamming into the Earth.

I screamed, the words barely audible over the chanting of the witches.

Bright light surrounded me, and it took me a second to understand it was me it came from. My entire body lit up like a freaking beacon. I shook my head and the pain the motion caused made bile rise up my throat. Swallowing it, I bit down on my tongue and tried to stay as calm as possible. The chanting intensified, and I blinked away the swarming darkness in my periphery to see symbols light up around me. I didn't remember learning these in my lessons with Luna. These were ancient runes, ones that have long been abandoned by the High Coven. The runes swirled around me in a tornado, and my hair whipped over my face, slashing at my skin.

My throat was on fire.

I opened my mouth to gulp in air, choking on it as the runes continued to swarm me.

Suddenly, it all stopped.

I rose up on my elbows and scanned the front yard. The bright, glowing runes circled me and created a barrier between me and the others. I found River in the crowd, his mouth opening and closing like he was saying something. I couldn't hear a word. A few feet from him, Peyton tried to rush toward me, but as soon as her body collided with the wall of runes, she was catapulted back. She landed in the crowd, her face red with anger. If I knew my best friend, she was probably cursing up a storm over there.

Brushing my hair off my face, I sat up, crossing my legs in a lotus pose. My eyes narrowed on a blue glow behind the circle, close to where Torine's house once stood. Oh my Goddess. She actually did it.

Shaking, I stretched out a finger in the direction of the opening portal.

Everyone but River turned around and cheers erupted from the front yard. I watched, a smile tugging at my lips, as several fae stepped through the portal and into our realm. Followed by a few more. They kept coming, filling up the space until I could barely make out their faces. There were so many magical people, it was hard to keep track.

"Come on," I whispered. "Come on."

My heart beat wildly in my chest and the back of my lids burned. I fisted my hands, waiting. Panic built up within me and I flicked my eyes to River's, my shoulders relaxing when he put his hand up slowly. *Calm down. They're going to make it.*

Another loud cheer ripped through the crowd and I followed everyone's gazes back to the portal. My body bristled, and I slumped in my rune prison when I saw Vic walk through the portal. Her back ramrod straight, she marched to join the other fae. I didn't fail to notice Solen walking beside her, their fingers entwined. My gaze traveled up their arms, noticing the matching symbols carved over their skin. Mate marks. Not the kind River and I shared, but similar. I smiled.

"Get it, girl."

Chewing on my bottom lip until I tasted blood, I waited.

For a moment, I thought we lost them, but then two more bodies pushed through the portal and I all but fell down in relief. Logan and Savannah rushed away from Faerie and joined the others seconds before the entire shadower community pounced on them. A few shifters hoisted Logan up and carried him around like a trophy, while Savannah chuckled, giving Morgan a tight hug. My face was soaking wet, and I swiped at the tears that refused to stop flowing with the back of my hand. My heart felt like it might explode in my chest.

I wanted so badly to celebrate with them.

I wanted to hug my brother.

I didn't want to be alone.

Nerves wracked my body as I pushed away from the ground, jumping up to stand. I ran to the barrier line, my palms pressing against the bright, glowing wall. "I changed my mind!" I screamed. "I don't want to forget this!"

River's palms flattened out, and he hovered them an inch off the barrier, his eyes wet. I pressed my palms to meet his and whispered, "I love you."

Though I couldn't hear him, I knew he said it back.

That was when everything went to hell in a hand basket.

The runes started to vibrate and rise higher. As they did, my insides felt like they were following them. I was suffocating, pressure unlike any I've felt before built up in my body, pushing its way through my skin. My legs gave way, and I dropped to my knees, bones turning to liquid. I tried to look at River, but all I could see was white light. Terror gripped my every cell, and I pressed my hands to my temples, screaming as the pressure grew until I could no longer bear it. Through slitted eyes, I watched Torine throw her hands in the air and direct the runes and the ball of energy they carried into the portal. I screamed as she threw my magic away. The portal swelled with it, eating it up like a hungry beast. The blue glow of the open doorway shimmered for a few moments before it closed in on itself, vanishing from view. The bomb was in Faerie and Faerie was gone.

A pop sounded in my head and suddenly, complete silence enveloped the space I crouched in.

One by one, I opened my hot and blurry eyes.

"What in the—"

"Babe?" River dropped to sit in front of me, his hands instantly warming my freezing fingers. "Are you okay?"

I shook my head, trying to recall the last few weeks. "I don't know. What happened?"

Pulling me into him, River rested my head on his shoulder and stroked my hair softly. "I'll explain everything. Right now, let's get you—"

"What the hell is that thing?" I pushed away from him, horrified at the sight of a giant, green-skinned man with purple horns staring at me. The man stood next to my half-brother, and they seemed chummy. Was no one else seeing this? Had I been drinking? I looked around the massive crowd surrounding us. *Are we at a costume party?*

My insides twisted and my brain fogged up. I tried to keep my eyes focused, but everything blurred at the edges. Confusion laced through my bones. Why couldn't I remember anything? And who were all these strange-looking creatures? I had so many questions, but I couldn't seem to form the words. It was as if my mouth refused to speak them. A few bodies parted ways, and I spotted a familiar face in the crowd. My mom walked toward us, something clutched in her fingers. Her hands shook as she lowered down to sit beside me, fingers stroking my hair to get it out of my sweaty face. "You okay, baby?"

Looking up at her, I whispered, "I don't feel so great."

"This should help," Mom said and pressed her hand to my chest.

A second later, I was out cold.

Chapter
Thirty-three

Billie

THREE MONTHS LATER...

he clock ticked so slowly, I thought I was going to die of old age before the bell signifying the end of school finally rang out. I grabbed my bag from under the wobbly desk and slung it over my shoulder, running out the door. Behind me, the rest of the students of Shadowhurst Academy followed suit, and we crashed into the packed hallway like a stampede of wild boars. Yells filled the area by the lockers where everyone gathered, reviewing their summer plans. We made it. Our last year at the school and then we were off to be so-called adults. The world was not ready for this group.

I passed a cluster of girls chatting about their perspective colleges and dread filled my gut. I was so not ready to leave. At least the school I picked was in Stamwick, and I could stay with Mom in her brand-new apartment downtown. I couldn't freaking wait. The Chandlers were nice enough to let me live in their guest house rent-free until the end of the school year, probably pitying my mom. Not that I could blame them; the woman did over a decade in jail for petty theft and was seriously trying way too hard to act like she was a well-to-do citizen. I mean seriously, my mom running an all-female tech startup? Who would have thought we'd live to see that?

Sometimes it made me laugh, but for the most part, I was just glad to have her back.

I crept by the principal's office and my traitorous eyes watered a little. *Get your act together, Billie! You can always come visit.*

It seemed like it was only yesterday that I moved to Shadowhurst. I still remembered how angry I was with my social workers for shipping me off here. One tiny mistake at the group home and they wrote me off. Granted, stealing and following in my mom's footsteps was probably what set them off in the first place. I knew that now, and I couldn't be more grateful for their decision.

If it wasn't for them, I never would have met—

"Yo, B! Over here!"

My body spun around to Peyton's voice, and a grin formed on my lips. To celebrate our freedom, my best friend opted to wear her flashiest outfit, and she looked like a peacock with her rainbow-dyed hair (a new style) and the sequin-covered oversized blazer in ombre orange (an old Halloween costume). Next to her, Morgan was dressed in a floral maxi dress, her red hair flowing over her shoulders. The two could not have been more opposite, and it was awesome.

Scanning the hallway, my eyes caught on Savannah and River chatting by his locker. My stomach did a somersault as

I hopped toward them, an invisible thread pulling me closer to my boyfriend. I couldn't believe our luck; we both got into Stamwick College. Leaving Shadowhurst—and Peyton, who decided to go to a local art college—was going to be hard enough, and I was glad I would have River with me so I didn't feel quite so alone.

"Hey, babe," River said when he saw me approach. His arm draped around me and I snuggled into his warm body, relishing in the moment. "Ready to go?"

"Not really," I admitted.

A fist bumped my side, and I turned to face Peyton. "Wanna go to Main Street and grab a coffee? Like old times?"

"Definitely!" Looking over River's shoulder, I locked eyes with Savannah. "You coming?"

"Nope. I have to go pack before we leave tonight. But you guys have fun!"

"What time do you leave?" I asked.

Savannah smiled wider than I'd seen her do in a while. "Flight is in a couple of hours," she answered, still beaming. "Logan set us up in a small villa for the first few days and then we're off to Italy to meet everyone. He said he has the whole thing planned."

River arched an eyebrow. "Naturally, you're going to be changing all his plans?"

"You got it!"

She waved, running off down the hallway while River shouted, "Call us when you get there!" at her disappearing back. I couldn't believe she was actually going through with it. I knew she and my half-brother were getting serious, but enough to take a year off college and travel the world together? Then again, Savannah Michaels was always way braver than I was. And the two of them were so cute together it was sickening. When Logan said he was going to be spending a lot of time traveling to catch up with his mother's side of the family, I think I knew deep down that Savannah was going with him. So when she told us last month she was hightailing it out of here for a life of adventure hanging out with Logan's eccentric family members, I wasn't too surprised.

I think I was more shocked to find out Logan took a DNA test and found a ton of random family all over the place. We're talking a *lot*, like in the hundreds. Most of them stayed in some commune in Europe. The way Logan described it when I talked to him last was they kept to themselves and did everything inside the commune. We're talking everything. His family had their own farms, their own school, everything one needed to survive. It all sounded very earth-loving to me. Which was why I was shocked Savannah wanted to be a part of it. But she seemed really excited, and I couldn't blame her for wanting to get out of Shadowhurst. Much like my brother, Savannah Michaels was made for a bigger life than this small town could provide. A part of me envied them for having so many new people to meet, but a bigger part of me was relieved it wasn't me.

I was quite happy in my little bubble, thank you very much.

"Earth to Beeeeeeeeee," Peyton sing-songed in my ear.

I shook off my wayward thoughts and looked at her. "Let's get out of here."

Main Street was the same concoction of locals and tourists, and I bumped at least ten shoulders before we even made it half the block. In the distance, I could see the sign for the Roasted Bean, the cafe we frequented a few times a week after school. There was already a lineup of students forming at the door, and I could hear their squeals all the way from here. Everyone was so eager for the summer. I couldn't blame them. Summers at Shadowhurst were the best. Lounging by Peyton's pool, parties at the quarry, I couldn't wait for all of it.

This summer was going to be amazing. Especially since Vic agreed to stay with me for a few weeks before she started school in the city. I wasn't sure how she'd do leaving Solen behind—the two were tied at the hip—but she said she needed girl time and I was more than happy to oblige. Besides, knowing them, they'd find a way to talk every minute of the day anyhow. It was strange to think they only met recently and yet were so close. Then again, River and I were pretty much the same so I couldn't complain.

His ears must have burned from me thinking of him because River chose that particular moment to tug on the sleeve of my leather jacket, a gift from mom after I lost the one I had most of my adult life. "I'm going to grab us a table while you guys get in line."

"I'll come with," Morgan said.

As the two of them shuffled away, I felt Peyton's eyes sear into me.

I side-glanced at her. "What?"

"Nothing," she said, biting her bottom lip. "I'm going to miss this next year."

My jaw tensed. "Me too. But you'll come visit us in

Stamwick all the time, right? When you're not with Morgan or busy with school, I mean."

"Obvi!" Peyton agreed. "Are you excited about living with your mom again?"

I bristled, adrenaline carving up my spine. "Honestly, I'm a little worried. The two of us haven't lived together since, well, since I was a kid. I hope we don't fight a lot."

"Oh, you will," my best friend teased. "That will be half the fun, though."

My head was suddenly full of worry and I tugged at the zipper of my jacket, yanking it up and down until it got stuck half-way.

"You okay, B?" Peyton asked.

"Huh? Oh, yep. All good." I looked around the street, the knot in my throat growing. "You ever feel like you're forgetting something? Something important, but obviously not, or else you'd remember."

For a moment, I thought I saw Peyton flinch, but she was back to her cheerful self in no time. Her arms looped around my waist, and she tugged me toward the cafe, grinning toothily. "You're probably nervous about college. Don't stress, girl. We got all summer to get wild before we have to grow our asses up. It's going to be epic!"

Chuckling, I let her drag me forward, eager to get a cup or two of sweet, sweet caffeine in me. For some reason, my head felt swollen and there was a pressure behind my temples that wasn't there before. I looked down at my fingers, waiting for... I'm not sure what. The hairs on the back of my neck stood on edge as we passed a storefront. I skidded to a stop, yanking Peyton with me.

Eyes traveling up to the metal sign hanging overhead, I

bit down on my tongue. "How come we never go here?" I asked.

"Crystal Cauldron?" Peyton's forehead creased. "It's mostly for tourists. I didn't think you were into witchy stuff."

I shook my head. "I'm not, I don't think." My eyes locked on the sign and I swiveled out of Peyton's arm. "I'm going to check it out while we wait for the drinks."

Peyton said something, but I didn't hear her because I was already through the door and squeezing into the tight space of the shop. A light jingle of a bell rang overhead as I stepped inside and shut the door behind me. Before me, a long and narrow room stretched farther than I imagined and I walked the length of it, gawking at the weird items on the shelves lining the walls. The smell of patchouli and beach wood permeated my senses, and I blinked my watering eyes, trying to stay focused. Slowly, I walked to the rear of the shop, where an ancient-looking woman in a flowing dress busied herself behind a glass counter.

When I approached, her eyes widened in recognition and I frowned. I had never seen this woman before in my life.

"Um, hi," I said awkwardly.

"Can I help you find anything?" the shop owner asked.

I glanced around, doubting I would need anything from this place. I had no interest in collecting any of the "magical" items the shop displayed. And yet...

"I'm not sure," I said. "I was passing by and thought to stop in. Interesting collection you have here."

The shop owner looked at me quizzically, her one eyebrow rising. Lips tugging, she flashed me the briefest of smiles before taking a few steps over to a necklace display sitting on the counter. Her index finger spun the circular stand, and she stopped it, landing on one necklace in particular. Yanking it off the display, she came back around and extended her hand. "Try this one," she said, holding out a pendant with a gorgeous, giant blue stone hanging off it.

"Oh, it's okay," I whispered. "I'm not really here to buy anything."

"It's on the house," the shop owner replied.

I backed away a foot, holding my hands up. "I couldn't. Though it is quite beautiful."

Smiling, the shop owner stretched her arm out further, accosting me with the pendant.

"It's not a bother, dear. The amethyst, it belongs with you."

What in the fresh hell? This woman was off her hinges and it was starting to freak me out big time. I wanted to argue, but something told me it would be no use. Glancing at the door, I realized I must have been gone way too long already. My eyes flicked to the pendant. If accepting this stranger's even stranger gift got me out of here without confrontation, I was willing to take the chance.

Briskly, I reached for the necklace and wrapped my hand over it.

The stone warmed in my palm and I yelped as the heat increased. My eyes widened, and I looked up at the shop owner, dread wracking my bones as the grin on her face spread. The heat in my hand moved up my arm, and I tried to pry my fingers apart to drop the pendant, but my body wouldn't cooperate. My teeth split, a scream hanging off my trembling lips.

I stammered backward, my shoulders colliding with a shelf. Crystals and bushels of herbs tumbled to the ground. I didn't care. My entire body felt like someone put a match to it. I shook my hand to free it of the amethyst. The headache building in my head exploded, and I slammed my head into the wall, my eyes rolling backward.

Suddenly, I saw it all.

The High Coven. The shadowers. The magic.

Everything I lost came crashing into me, rearranging my entire existence to make space for itself. Tears streamed down my cheeks and my heart beat so fast, it was about to rip out of my ribcage. My thighs quivered, and I squeezed the side of the shelf to keep myself from falling down. Eyes meeting Miss Broussard's burning gaze, I froze in my spot. "How?"

"Some magic is much too powerful to be erased," the shop owner whispered.

My chin dipped, and I gasped as shadows enveloped my hands and arms. *My* shadows. *My* magic. I was back!

"My mom doesn't work for a startup," I said.

Miss Broussard laughed, her voice like a wind chime. Man, I missed this woman. "She's a high priestess now. Took her oath last month."

An ache reverberated in my gut. Beatrix took a priestess oath and I missed it. I hated to think about what else I missed in the last three months. My breath caught in my throat. "Oh my goddess," I whispered. "Logan's family in Europe... I'm so dumb. He's over there with the fae, isn't he? And Savannah is on her way to help."

"Yes, yes they are. Your brother is quite the leader," the shop owner filled in the gaps. "After the fae crossed over, he helped them set up a community where they could flourish without imposing on humans. Their magic is no longer what it used to be in Faerie, but they make do with what they have. I hear even the fire fae are thriving."

My eyes bulged out of their sockets. "I honestly thought Logan would be glad to be free of his king duties."

"Quite the opposite, I believe," Miss Broussard said. "I think you'll find your brother found his purpose in life. Both here and in Faerie."

Tears burned the rear of my lids. "I really need to call him." Then adding, "And Savannah. She should get an Emmy for her performance this last little while. I seriously fell for the long-lost family story."

"Correct me if I'm wrong, but I believe that was the point."

"I guess," I mused. "I hate how much I missed."

The shop owner stepped around the counter and came to stand beside me, her thin arm wrapping over my shoulder. "No need to dwell on the past," she said. "You have your entire life ahead of you, Billie. With or without magic, those you love are always near, and you cannot miss that which is right there at your fingertips."

Grinning, I gasped as a thought flashed in my mind. "I can't wait to tell River and Peyton!"

"Best get on that," Miss Broussard said, patting my back. "Come see me on your way home. I'll put together a few things for you to take home."

Yelling a quick *thank you* over my shoulder, I bolted out of the Crystal Cauldron, the door swinging behind me. I pushed through bodies, making my way to the cafe. When I reached it, my hair was a wild mess and there were black lines of mascara down my face that made it appear as though I was on my way to fight an ancient battle. Panting, I found my friends at a small table in the corner of the cafe. My heart jolted in my chest.

I stalked toward them, their eyes bulging as they took in the state I was in.

"Babe? What's going on?"

Glancing from River to Peyton to Morgan, I sucked in a long, steady breath and smiled. My palms pressed to the marble tabletop, and I summoned the shadows, making them dance across my skin while angling my body so that only our group could see them. Everyone gasped, their faces ashen from the shock of my magic having returned.

I chuckled, pulling the shadows back into my body. Pulling up a chair, I took a giant drag of the iced latte River ordered for me and sighed. "You're right, Peyton," I said, winking. "This is going to be epic."

ACKNOWLEDGMENTS

The journey is over... or is it?

I can't believe this is the final book of the Shadowhurst Mysteries series. It seems it was only yesterday that I sat down to plot Witch of Shadows, the excitement of a new adventure bubbling to the surface. Eight books in, and that excitement remains.

A massive thank you to Oliver-Heber Books and the brilliant team that helped make this book a reality. Kate, your feedback was incremental in making this book the strongest ending for Billie and her friends. And Tanya, thank you for always being there to answer questions or help guide me along the way. OHB—you are amazing!

To Scott, thank you for putting up with my wild rambling and helping me brainstorm myself out of a block. You are the best partner in crime I could ask for.

Mom and dad, you are the reason I found the courage to start writing. Thank you for your support throughout this journey.

And to my beautiful and wild daughter—chase your dreams! I am so proud of the person you are becoming and hope to do you proud every day.

Finally, to you, my lovely reader. Without you, this series would not exist and I thank you from the bottom of my heart for sticking with it. You are the reason I sit down and write every day.

Stay magical!

ABOUT THE AUTHOR

A.N. Sage is a bestselling, award-winning author of mystery and fantasy novels. She has spent most of her life waiting to meet a witch, vampire, or at least get haunted by a ghost. In between failed seances and many questionable outfit choices, she has developed a keen eye for the extra-ordinary.

A.N. spends her free time reading and binge-watching television shows in her pajamas. Currently, she resides in Toronto, Canada with her husband who is not a creature of the night and their daughter who just might be.

A.N. Sage is a Scorpio and a massive advocate of leggings for pants.

For more books and updates:
www.ansage.ca

Connect on social media:
Facebook Group:
facebook.com/groups/945090619339423/
Instagram:
instagram.com/a.n.sage/
Twitter:
twitter.com/ANsageWrites
Facebook:

facebook.com/ansagewrites

Pinterest:

pinterest.ca/ansagewrites

Goodreads:

goodreads.com/author/show/18901100.Alexis_N_Sage

Amazon:

amazon.com/author/a.n.sage